FIRE

BOOK ONE OF THE ELEMENTS OF THE UNDEAD SERIES

WILLIAM
ESMONT

This book is a work of fiction. Names, characters, places and incidents are products of the author's imagination or are used fictitiously. Any resemblance to actual events or locals or persons, living or dead, is entirely coincidental.

Print edition April 2011

ISBN: 978-0-9828758-3-4

www.williamesmont.com
Cover by www.streetlightgraphics.com

Other works by William Esmont:

The Patriot Paradox

Self Arrest

Getting a raw story out of my head and onto paper is only the first step in a months-long process before it becomes a story worth reading. Countless people are involved in the process, and they all deserve a mention. First, I'd like to thank my wife Robin. She puts up with the countless hours I spend hunched over my laptop, writing and researching, the endless discussions of characters and plot, cover designs, and most of all, the periodic bouts of self-doubt inherent in such an endeavor. Next, I'd like to thank my beta readers: Chris Merhige, Mark Jaggers, Don Query, and Dan Moore – you guys are lifesavers! You were gracious enough to read my mostly-finished manuscript and provide brutally honest feedback. It's a better book because of you. Next up is Glendon Haddix of Streetlight Graphics. Glendon came up with the cover design of Fire, as well as the interior layout of the print version. He's a master at taking a sparse description and turning it into something that leaps from the virtual bookshelves, grabs potential readers by the neck and screams, "Read me, damn it!" Thanks, Glendon! And last but not least, my editor, Lynn O'Dell. Lynn, from "Red Adept Editing Services," took my self-edited manuscript, complete with changes from my beta readers and sanded off the rough edges, swapped chapters around, and generally made it a better book. Thank you, Lynn!

A note about the geography: Although the story is mostly set in Tucson, Arizona, I did take some creative liberties with the geography to make it work for the story. For those of you familiar with the Tucson area, Scorpion Canyon is indeed Sabino Canyon. If you've never been there, you should pay it a visit. It's beautiful.

The Undoing

Things fall apart; the centre cannot hold;
Mere anarchy is loosed upon the world,
The blood-dimmed tide is loosed, and everywhere
The ceremony of innocence is drowned;
William Butler Yeats, The Second Coming

One

Megan Pritchard stretched and yawned. She was only two hours into the graveyard shift, and she had already served three customers. The first had been a laid-back, beer-drinking trucker, the second, a German who reeked of tequila and had trouble keeping it up, and the last, a wild-eyed, fifty-something man who smelled like a dirty ashtray and wouldn't take no for an answer. Number four, another trucker, was in the bathroom washing up. She sighed and ran her hand across the bed, smoothing the comforter. The toilet flushed.

Any second now.

She arranged herself in a seductive pose, angling her leg to show a hint of pubic hair and squeezing her breasts together like her roommate Heather had taught her. The door opened, and a bear of a man strode in wearing only a stupid grin and a faded black cowboy hat.

"You ready to play, baby?" he drawled. West Texas.

Megan smiled and beckoned with her right index finger. She looked at his crotch. "I'm not sure I can handle you, Ray."

He blushed at the lie. In truth, she was disappointed in what he brought to the bedroom. At six-foot-three and two hundred and sixty pounds, she figured he'd be packing something more than the tiny sausage poking from the nest of gray hair between his legs. *Whatever. I get paid either way.*

Ray stepped toward the bed, but she held up her palm. "Hold on, big boy. We need to settle up first."

His smile faltered for a heartbeat, then was replaced by a boyish flash of uncertainty. He recovered quickly. "Right. Of course." He picked up his pants from the wooden footstool beside the bathroom and dug out his wallet. Counting out a thick stack of twenties, he placed them on the bedside dresser and took a step back.

Megan scooped up the cash and inspected it, rubbing each bill between her thumb and forefinger to verify its authenticity. She raised an eyebrow as she realized there was an extra hundred dollar bill on top of the pile. "What's this?"

Ray leered. "A little incentive..."

The bills went into the lockbox bolted to the headboard. She winked. "We're all set."

At a hair under five-foot-seven, Megan had the bright-eyed, girl-next-door look that turned men into drooling school boys. She had her mother's genes to thank for her figure and her father's for her lustrous black hair, her perky, upturned nose and luminous gray eyes.

She waved him to the fake French-baroque dresser beside her bed, and pulled open the top drawer, revealing a kaleidoscope-colored collection of condoms.

"Take your pick."

He scratched his chin in thought, and then chose one. Magnum. Of course.

Megan always kept a healthy supply of the king-sized condoms on hand. It was all about the ego; she had learned that early on. And if that's what got him off, who was she to complain?

She held out her hand. "I'll take care of that."

Ray surrendered the package. With an expert touch, she tore open the wrapper and slid the rubber between her teeth and lips. A few seconds later, he was wrapped and ready to go.

She gave him a few quick strokes and pulled him onto the bed. Gazing into his eyes, she asked, "Where do you want me?"

"Let's start out regular and see how things go."

"Sure." She drew him in. This one's going to be quick, she thought. Hoped.

Top.

Bottom.

Behind.

Top. Again.

Pop!

Another two hundred dollars in her bank account. Easy as pie.

He rolled off and collapsed beside her with a contented smile plastered across his fleshy face.

"Better?" she asked.

Ray grunted and started to check his watch, but she caught his arm and gave his knuckles a kiss, distracting him. Her room, like all the others in the brothel, was a clock-free cocoon, engineered to support an ancient fantasy. With no way to tell time, customers tended to be far more willing to pay for more when it ran out.

He was playing with himself, rubbing against her leg.

What's this?

She glanced at the digital timer tucked out of Ray's direct line of sight beside the bed. He had three minutes left in his twenty-minute session. A second round wasn't out of the question, but it required more cash, something she suspected he didn't have.

"Let's cuddle," she said, resting her head on his chest. His chest hairs tickled her ear.

"Come on, sweetheart. What do you think the extra hundred was for?"

Megan batted her eyelashes at him, put her hand on his, and mirrored his stroking motion.

Gotta run down the clock, she thought.

"If you had a little more money..."

Ray cast his eyes away, mumbling something under his breath. She moved to get up from the bed. He touched her elbow, a desperate, but tender, gesture. "I'm all tapped out..."

Despite her better judgment, Megan felt a twinge of pity. He seemed like a wannabe high roller, the kind of guy that hit it big every once in a while, but was never able to keep it going.

She softened. "I'll tell you what, we only have a few minutes left…"

"Really?" He perked up.

"How about I..." She nudged his hand aside and took its place. Slow at first, then she picked up the pace as his time grew short.

Ray closed his eyes. "Don't stop..." She counted in her head: Five, Four, Three. He finished at Two.

He exhaled, long and slow. "You're amazing, baby, you know that?"

Megan pecked him on the forehead. "I do." She scooted to the edge of the bed and dangled her feet over, searching for her slippers. "It's time to go now, big guy." She gave his belly a playful pat.

Ray let out a groan of protest, but hoisted himself up and joined her. He gathered his clothes and dressed quickly before slinking out of the room and back to whatever life he led outside.

Megan fell back on the bed and lay staring at the ceiling, counting the peaks in the acoustic popcorn finish. She only had a few minutes to clean the room and prepare for the next lineup.

As she was about to get up, a stabbing pain blossomed deep within her gut. She winced, and her eyes teared up. Trying in vain to hold back the inevitable, her hand flew to her mouth.

She barely made it to the bathroom before the contents of her stomach erupted from her mouth in a hot torrent, splattering the rim of the toilet with the half-digested remains of the burrito she had eaten hours earlier. The nausea rolled through her like a raging tsunami; hot waves of uncontrollable agony drained her energy, leaving her whimpering on the floor like a young child.

And then it was gone. Her stomach stopped heaving, her vision cleared, and she felt human again. It was as if the sickness had happened to someone else.

Megan got to her feet and stared down at the toilet in disgust. She pulled a towel from under the sink and wiped her mouth. The room stunk. Rolling out a handful of toilet paper, she wiped down the edges of the toilet, then flushed the sopping paper and floating clumps of half-digested food to oblivion.

Her throat burned, and her diaphragm ached from all of the heaving. She went to the sink, washed her hands, and rinsed her mouth, gargling afterward with a shot of peppermint Scope to banish the vile aftertaste. It didn't work. She gargled another shot. *That's better.*

She turned on the bathroom fan to suck out the smell of puke, and then padded back into the bedroom.

The house doorbell chimed.

Damn it. Already?

With a tired sigh, Megan stripped the cum-soaked sheets from the bed and stuffed them in the hamper, preparing the room for her next client.

Two

Alicia tucked an errant strand of strawberry-blond hair behind her ear and bumped the drawer closed with her hip.

"Seventeen, eighteen, and nineteen is twenty," she said, handing a fistful of bills and coins to the frazzled housewife on the other side of the counter. The woman shot her a grim smile and pushed her cart into the stream of people heading for the store exit.

Alicia checked her watch. Five minutes until break time. God I need to get out of here. She glanced over her shoulder at the next cashier station. Her best friend Brittany frowned back at her and mouthed the word 'help!'

Four minutes. Fuck it. I'm out of here. She reached up and flipped off her light, signaling a closed lane. She spun and started walking toward the door.

"Wait! Miss!" Despite her desire to keep walking, her responsible side took over. She stopped and turned.

"I'm on break now. One of the other lanes can help you." She held firm.

"But you were open just a second ago," the customer whined, gesturing at the light.

"I'm sorry," Alicia said, trying to sound sincere. She had no intention of sacrificing her precious fifteen minutes for this pushy bitch.

Technically, she was required to take her break in the rear of the store in the kitchen area, but she wanted to spend her time somewhere a little more interesting. She waved at Dave, the receipt checker, as she breezed past. He ignored her. Dork.

Her Subaru was in the far corner of the parking lot, out of sight of the surveillance cameras. She beeped the car as she approached, and the headlights flashed once.

Once safely ensconced in the car, she popped open the center console, took out her iPod, turned it on, and cranked up the volume. As an afterthought, she pushed the central door lock, sealing herself in. Digging around in her backpack, she pulled out a small Ziploc bag. With dismay, she realized her pot supply was almost exhausted. The ounce she had purchased only a week before was no more than seeds and a few lonely buds. Shit.

She broke the seal on the bag with the tip of her finger and inhaled, reveling in the pungent aroma of the remains of her Super Skunk. She reached into her backpack again and pulled out her bowl, a compact swirled-glass favorite she had had since junior high school.

Someone rapped on her window, and she jumped in surprise. Cupping her pipe in one hand, she put on her most innocent face and peeked out, prepared for the worst.

Fuck me. She relaxed. Brittany stood outside the car grinning like a maniac. Alicia exhaled a sigh of relief and pressed the unlock button.

Brittany slid in beside her. "Thanks. Can you believe the crowds today?"

With a noncommittal shrug, Alicia locked the doors and retrieved her pot. She chose the plumpest bud from her bag and crammed it into her bowl. "Sucks in there." She lit up.

Brittany eyed her. "It does. I couldn't take it anymore."

Alicia snorted, smoke jetting from her nose in twin streams and passed the pipe. They spent the next ten minutes smoking and refilling until only shake remained in the baggie, and they had run out of things to talk about. Alicia laughed to herself.

"What?" Brittany asked, tapping the ashes of the bowl into an empty Diet Coke can.

Alicia shook her head. "It's nothing." She checked the clock through heavy-lidded eyes. Three minutes until her break was over. Her life was supposed to have started by now. Instead, here she was, stuck in this shitty Costco in Tempe.

"Are you ready?" Brittany asked, shattering Alicia's reverie.

"Sure. I guess." She wasn't. She could spend all day out here.

She stuffed her pipe and the empty Ziploc into the bottom of her backpack, tucking them under a spare pair of panties. "Okay. Let's go."

The girls got out of the car, surrounded by a billowing cloud of smoke, and began the long walk across the hot parking lot. As they neared the front door, Alicia stopped and took Brittany by the elbow. "Do you ever think about leaving here? I mean…"

Brittany gave her a puzzled look. "Not really... Why? What's wrong?"

Alicia shuffled her feet. "I'm just…tired of this place." She looked at the ground.

Brittany laughed. "You're moody because you're stoned. You always get like this." She had a point. Brittany arched a perfect eyebrow. "Are you going out tonight?"

Alicia shrugged. "I don't know. It depends—"

Brittany cut her off. "Call me if you do. I want to get out for a little while."

"I will."

They entered the store and went their separate ways. *Three more hours,* Alicia thought with a pained expression.

Three

Jack leaned on his shovel and ran the back of his hand across his brow, wiping off the accumulated sweat. He stole a glance at his wife Becka and waited in silence as she dumped a shovelful of dirt. "Something to drink?"

She dropped her shovel with a *thud.* "I thought you'd never ask."

Jack groaned. His arms tingled, and his shoulders burned. He needed a glass of tea and a few minutes to relax if he had any hope of finishing the job today. *Or maybe even a beer.*

"Okay. I'll be back in a minute." He sank his shovel into a mound of dirt and took off across the yard toward the front porch.

The hole, seven feet long by six wide and a little over a foot deep at the moment, was intended for a koi pond, a surprise birthday present for their twin daughters, Maddie and Ellie. As usual, they didn't have enough money to hire an excavator, so this had become yet one more in an endless procession of do-it-yourself projects.

The idea had been born two weeks before on a routine trip to Home Depot. He was browsing the tool aisle when she called out to him. "Jack?"

"Huh?" He held a shovel in each hand, trying to decide if the shiny stainless steel model warranted an extra twenty dollars.

"I've got an idea," she said, her voice full of mischief. *Uh oh.* He knew that tone. *Trouble.* He gave her his attention. "You know how the girls are into fish…"

Jack nodded. The girls were in the midst of their first small pet phase. From bettas to goldfish to species he couldn't even pronounce, the house looked like an aquarium, with tanks covering every horizontal surface. Becka's idea consisted of a second shovel—stainless, he insisted—along with a large, black plastic pond insert and a cheap solar pump.

He suppressed a groan. "Are you sure? What about winter? Won't it freeze?"

Becka rolled her eyes, took the shovel, and threw it in their cart.

Half an hour later, they were on their way home with the tools in the bed of his pickup along with an eight-by-ten pond.

He strolled into the kitchen, got two glasses from the cabinet over the sink, and then went to the refrigerator. A refreshing wave of chilled air washed over him when he opened the French doors. *Damn....* He held them open and wedged his entire six-foot-two frame in as close as possible, savoring the coolness. He stayed in that position for a full minute, eyes half-closed, fantasizing about a mythical afternoon of leisure, a distant memory from the time before the girls. Finally satisfied, he took a half-full pitcher of iced tea from the top shelf and filled their glasses.

On the way out, he grabbed two oatmeal cookies from a plate on the counter, stuffing one into his mouth and pinching the other between the fingers of his free hand. Pushing through the front door, he smiled. Becka was lying in the grass, her eyes closed, her legs dangling into the hole. Covered in dirt and grime, with her dirty-blonde hair plastered against her head, she looked at peace with herself, completely in her element. Her white cotton halter top, the torn one she always wore when working outside in the summer, clung to the curves of her body, leaving little to his imagination. He descended the stairs and crossed the yard with a lascivious grin, fantasizing about what he was going to do with her later in the evening after they put the girls down. That was, if he could stay awake after all this digging. Becka heard him approach and opened her eyes. He handed her a tea and the uneaten cookie.

"Thanks." She touched the cold drink to her cheek and smiled, glowing.

He drained his own glass and let out a growling belch.

"Excuse me," he said, embarrassed.

Becka giggled.

Jack touched the still-cool glass to his cheek. "I should have brought the pitcher out. I'm still thirsty. "

Becka sipped again and waved at the house with her free hand. Jack took off.

~~~

Becka put her empty glass on a level spot and climbed back into the pit. They had to go down at least one more foot before declaring victory. It would be easy if it weren't for the damned roots, some the size of her forearm, several even larger. She still couldn't believe they came from the old cottonwood stump. Jack had laughed off her concerns at first, easily slicing through a bundle with the point of his shovel. But they kept appearing, as if the ground was determined to see them fail.
~~~

After three miserable hours and six inches of progress, she had asked "Do you want to try digging somewhere else?"

Jack was adamant. "No. This is the best spot in the yard. Plus, we're outside the main fence—which is what we wanted."

As they dug deeper, the roots multiplied. Becka estimated they had spent at least half of their time so far cutting the damned things. A testament to their efforts, a giant pile of shredded bark and root bits teetered beside the hole. They were committed.

She checked her watch. *Four thirty*. The twins were due to return at six. She shook her head in dismay. This won't be done in an hour. Maybe not in ten...

She considered calling Jack's mom and asking if she could keep the kids for a couple more hours, but decided it wasn't worth the hassle. It almost never was with her mother-in-law.

Becka resumed digging. She wedged her shovel under a particularly stubborn rootball, and leaned on the handle. Throwing her entire body into the effort, she hopped up and down, grunting like a wounded animal. The root popped out, but the shovel kept going, plunging deep before stopping abruptly with a leg-numbing clang.

"What the...?" She knelt and began sifting through the crumbly soil with her gloved hands, sweeping the dirt into a pile behind her.

"What's that?"

She nearly jumped out of her skin. "Jack! You surprised me!" She pointed at the thing she had uncovered. "I found something!"

"No shit?" Placing the pitcher on the ground, he climbed in beside her and started to help. Jack scratched his head and stood. Listening intently, he stomped hard on the flat metal surface. "Sounds hollow," he said, perplexed. "I bet we've got an old oil tank here."

Becka didn't have words to express her frustration. She glared at the new obstacle, fuming inside. This was supposed to be easy.

Four

Megan scrunched her eyes shut, willing herself to sleep. It didn't work. She was too damned hot. With a frustrated groan, she kicked out from under the sheet and padded across the trailer to the ancient air conditioner. She jabbed the power button, and the machine rattled to life.

On the way back to bed, she snatched the television remote from the coffee table. Her roommate Heather had gone out of town, which meant Megan had the entire trailer to herself. Usually this would be cause for celebration, but for some reason this morning, Megan craved company, wanted to talk to someone real.

The next five days were wide open, her first vacation in over six months, and she planned to use the time to her full advantage. She had a ticket in her purse to Tucson, where her sister lived. All that stood between her and her much-deserved break was the hour-long drive into Vegas. Her thoughts drifted to Chloe. Married with three children and a house in the suburbs, Chloe's lifestyle was the polar opposite of Megan's. Despite their differences, the sisters remained close. Megan played the role of favorite aunt to her nieces and nephew, showering them with gifts and treating them like the children she hoped to have some day.

She turned her attention to the television. *Infomercial.* Flipping through the channels, she settled on a documentary about supervolcanoes in Wyoming. That kind of thing fascinated her. She crawled back on the bed and cranked up the volume. Sleep should be close—she hoped. The Xanax she had popped half an hour ago was already nibbling at the fringe of her consciousness, sanding the rough edges off the night and turning the world into a soft and fuzzy place.

Another difference from Chloe. *Or maybe not.* Kids seemed the perfect justification for a discreet Xanax habit. She chuckled to herself, amused at their unlikely similarities. She didn't enjoy using the little blue pills, quite the contrary. But they sure took the edge off after a long night on her back. Anyone who said you could fuck for a living without some sort of self-medication was full of shit in Megan's book.

Someone knocked on the door. "Yeah? Come in!"

The door swung open and Samantha Cantor, her boss, slipped inside. She nudged the door closed with her heel. Megan sat up. "Sam! Hey! What are you doing here?"

"Have you seen the news yet, Megan?" Sam asked.

Megan cringed. "No. Why? Is something going on?" The last time someone had asked her that was the day the International Space Station had been destroyed by an errant satellite, killing everyone on board.

Sam walked over and made a spot for herself on the edge of the bed. She took the remote and flipped to CNN. Red banners and scrolling text screaming "Breaking News" blanketed the screen. A live shot from a helicopter hovered in the center. The camera jiggled and zoomed several times before finally stabilizing on a crowded street corner.

Megan stared in disbelief as people dashed in and out of the camera's view, colliding with each other as they raced in every direction. In some cases, they appeared to be wrestling, locked in a gruesome struggle for an unseen prize. The aerial camera focused on a young mother and her infant as a man tackled them from behind, pushing them into the street. As Megan and Sam watched, a speeding police cruiser, lights flashing, drove over all three, swerved out of control, and crashed into the rear of a UPS truck. The camera zoomed back out.

"Oh, my God!" Sam exclaimed.

Megan was confused. The coverage had the vibe of a street shot from some third-world hellhole. Desperate to find the ubiquitous robed men with chicken-scratched signs, she scanned the crowd, but only saw people that looked like herself—like her neighbors back home.

The scene shifted and the profile of the Transamerica Pyramid filled the background. A pall of thick, oily smoke clung to the horizon, blanketing the city with a viscous fog. "That's San Francisco." She gulped.

The video feed shrank to a small box in the lower left of the screen and was replaced by a shot of a man with a close-trimmed beard.

"This is Richard Mosby reporting from Washington. The president has declared a national state of emergency given the current events in San Francisco, Washington, and Miami. A press conference is scheduled for the top of the hour. CNN will have live coverage. Please stay tuned for the latest updates."

Megan nudged the volume down. "What's he talking about? I don't understand."

Sam coughed. "No one knows. It came out of nowhere...the first symptoms start like the flu. Within a couple of hours, people begin to change; they become violent, attacking everyone around them..."

Megan flipped to another news channel. Same thing, different reporters. She grabbed her mobile phone, punched in Chloe's number, then put the phone to her ear.. She frowned and checked the screen. "It's not working. I don't have a signal."

Sam gave her a sad nod. "They've been down for hours. Vegas, too."

A chill ran through her body, making her shiver. She stared at the screen, willing the signal bars to appear, but they didn't.

Megan took her laptop from the nightstand and opened her Instant Messenger program. Her sister wasn't online. Switching to email, she banged out a quick message, asking her to call.

She looked at Sam. "What do we do?"

"Vegas seemed fine, at least a few hours ago." Sam had been in Vegas the night before negotiating with a strip club owner about a promotional tie-in with the brothel. Sam shrugged and sniffled. "Anyway, I wanted to make sure you knew what was going on. I know you have plans to fly out of Vegas this afternoon... You may want to reconsider."

Megan got up and went to the window. She peered out, squinting into the sun. Everything appeared normal. Red dirt and rocks stretched as far as she could see. Scrub grass and tumbleweed cooked in the harsh sunlight.

Sam cleared her throat. "I'm heading back into Vegas to get some supplies. Do you want to come along?"

Megan turned around. "I don't think that's such a good idea, Sam. What if it's reached Vegas?"

Sam leaned away and coughed into her hand, a wet, raspy sound like an old, dry chainsaw. "I know. I thought of that, but our regular delivery arrives tomorrow and we're low on everything. If they don't show..."

Megan understood her concerns. She shared them. Without their weekly supplies, they wouldn't survive for long. Life in the desert was unforgiving this time of year with temperatures soaring into the 120s and no rain to speak of. She thought of her last shift and shuddered. Twelve clients in all, breathing on her, her sweat mingling with theirs. Inside of her. Her heart beat faster; her stomach churned. Megan took a deep breath, trying to calm herself. *She didn't feel sick.*

Sam picked up on her consternation. "What's wrong?"

"Nothing." Megan shook her head.

Sam patted her on the hand and got to her feet. "I'm sure it will all be fine. These things happen…" Her first step was unsteady, as if she had forgotten how to walk. Sweat poured from her brow, falling to the floor in fat drops. Giant stains blossomed from nowhere in the pits of her arms.

Megan straightened, putting a hand out to Sam. "Are you okay?"

As she watched, the color drained from Sam's cheeks, leaving her face a pasty gray with blood vessels visibly throbbing slowly beneath translucent skin.

As if on autopilot, Sam took another step before she faltered again. She pitched face-first into the narrow gap beside the bed, swiping Megan's alarm clock on the way down and setting it off. Megan sat in shocked silence, unable to believe what was happening in front of her. The alarm blared. Shit! She leaped across the room and attempted to pull Sam up, but she couldn't get leverage. The older woman was wedged in, pinned tight at her shoulders.

Megan snaked her hand to Sam's neck and checked for a pulse. Nothing. She tried the other side, but got the same result. *Oh, shit.*

Five

Four o'clock. Come on, four o'clock.

Alicia had only one hour left in her shift. Her buzz had worn off a while ago, leaving her tired, cranky, and craving a nap. She couldn't keep her eyes off the cheap digital clock attached to the top of her register, checking it every time she opened the drawer, and again when she slammed it closed. "Shitty economy," she muttered under her breath.

"Excuse me?" her current customer, a stylish, middle-aged woman with perfect bangs and a fat glittering rock on her left hand asked.

"I'm sorry. It's nothing. I'm babbling. I've had a bad day."

"I understand. I was your age once."

Alicia smiled despite herself. *This biddy has a sense of humor.* She reached for the first item on the conveyer belt, a giant bottle of Vodka. Curiosity got the better of her. "Big party?"

The woman nodded, fine strands of hair dancing on her forehead. "Yes. My son is graduating from the community college tomorrow."

Alicia perked up. "Which one?"

"City."

"No way." She stopped the conveyor belt. "I know some people over there."

"His name is Chaz. Chaz Perkins."

A hot flash of anger coursed through Alicia. She broke eye contact, glanced away, and tried to steady herself.

She had met Chaz a year ago at a friend's house. He had shown up with one of Alicia's friends and brought along a good friend of his own—a fat sack of weed. The late-spring party had started in mid-afternoon and raged into the night, providing ample time for Alicia to get way too messed up. She outdid herself, dipping into Chaz's stash over and over, chasing the perfect high. She had awakened the next morning in the back of his Grand Cherokee.

Sun beamed on her face, making her sweat. The air stank, a toxic mixture of stale pot, beer, and rancid body odor. Worst of all, she was naked from the waist down, and her pants were missing. Her recollection of the previous night fuzzed out sometime around sunset. Looking at Chaz snoring contentedly beside her, she couldn't fathom what she had been thinking. An oafish, clumsy boy, he had nothing going for him beyond a bottomless stash of weed.

She found her shorts wadded up on the front passenger seat and slipped into them as quietly as she could. Then she crawled out of the truck and dashed down the street to her car.

Later that day, she had gone to the drugstore and picked up two doses of the morning after pill, just in case. She was a ball of nerves as she waited in her doctor's office a few weeks later, convinced she had caught some horrible disease from Chaz. She got lucky, though, and received a clean bill of health.

She had never spoken to him again, had almost forgotten about the incident until this moment. She tried to smile. "I don't know him. Sorry."

"Well, it's going to be a big party. If you're looking for something to do, here's the address." The woman tore a slip of paper from her checkbook and started scribbling.

"Thanks," Alicia said, biting back her disgust as she took the paper to be polite. Out of the corner of her eye, she noticed the next customer in line glaring at her. She smiled in return.

Finally, she scanned the woman's last item, a carton of toothbrushes, and pushed the *Total* button.

"Joan," the woman said as she handed over her American Express. *She doesn't give up.*

Alicia swiped the card. "Nice to meet you. I'm Alicia." She studied Joan's face while the transaction processed. Up close, she looked like she took care of herself. Early forties, maybe forty-five, about her mom's age, Alicia guessed. And those bangs—*just fabulous*. She had to fight the urge to ask the name of her hairdresser.

A commotion erupted near the return counter. A young man, *the cart jockey*, she thought, tore through the entrance, his feet slipping and sliding on the polished concrete floor.

"They're coming!" People stared at him for a moment, and then returned to their business.

Alicia made eye contact. *Big mistake.* He dashed to her station, grabbed her by the shoulders, and shook her. "You have to get out of here! Now! They're in the lot. They'll be inside any minute!"

Something dripped on her upper arm. He was bleeding on her. "Eww!" She shook him off and pointed at the wound. "Are you okay? Did you cut yourself?"

"No! I'm fine. But that's what I'm trying to tell you! They're coming!" He turned and raced away, bumping into her next customer and spilling her cart in the process. Someone outside screamed, causing everyone to crane their heads, searching for the source.

Now Alicia was curious. She took her register keys and went to investigate. Other people, both customers and employees, were drifting in the same direction, drawn by the unexpected drama. When she rounded the corner and was able to see outside, Alicia felt her understanding of the world rip loose and slide away, a little earthquake in her mind.

Across the lot, less than thirty feet away, a man was on his knees, bent over another person, ripping and tearing at their throat. He was pulling enormous, bloody chunks of meat into his mouth and inhaling them like a wild animal.

"Is that real?" Joan asked from beside her.

Alicia had forgotten about her. She shrugged. This was Tempe after all. Anything was possible. Where's a damn manager when you need one? She cast about, searching for one. A giant hand brushed her shoulder, and the next thing she knew, Big Don Harding, her supervisor, nudged her to the side and pushed past.

Her stomach knotted up. She tasted bile, as if she was going to vomit. "You can't go outside," she said.

He gave her a stern glare. "And why not?"

"I…"

He rolled his eyes. "Come on, Alicia. I'm sure it's some kind of movie promotion or something. Whatever it is, they can't do it here. Not without getting approval from Corporate." He started for the exit.

Alicia turned her attention back to the men in the parking lot. The first man was standing and staring at the people clustered around the door. Blood and gore dripped from his face, coating his chest in Technicolor-red. He chewed intently and swallowed the last bits of his meal.

She glanced behind him at the body on the ground. It twitched. Alicia did a double take. She could have sworn the man on the ground had just moved. That's impossible. As she stared in disbelief, one of his feet kicked out. Then, with a groan, he rolled over and struggled to his feet.

Alicia swallowed hard. The man's throat was in tatters, the fleshy parts chewed to the point where his vertebrae showed through, glistening white, slick, and greasy. His head tilted at an odd angle, the destroyed muscles of his neck barely supporting the weight of his head.

Customers began backing from the open door, slowly at first, but then with a rising sense of urgency. Alicia sensed the fear sweeping through the crowd; it was an electric current triggering a full-blown panic in the blink of an eye.

"I don't like this," she said. "I think you should close up."

Don was paralyzed, seemingly torn between his duty to the store and his instinct for self-preservation. The man with no throat turned his head, tracking slowly across the front of the building. He stopped and focused on Alicia, his empty gaze boring into her. He began to moan, the sound increasing in intensity until it became a full-fledged roar. He took a shaky step toward her. The other man licked his lips and followed.

Alicia screamed, "Close the fucking doors, Don!"

Six

Cesar smiled, recalling his first journey north—the heat, the people, the sense of hope laced with desperation. What he remembered most vividly was the overwhelming satisfaction of embarking on a grand adventure, of shrugging off his old life and gambling everything on his ability to survive the wilderness and avoid the *patrulla fronteriza,* the border patrol.

The path undulated like an angry serpent, shattered red and brown rocks fading away to smooth desert floor before abruptly returning. Pebble-filled arroyos crisscrossed the landscape at random intervals, torturing him with constant reminders of nonexistent water.

He got a small sense of comfort from being on this path again, from knowing he wasn't alone in his quest for a better life. The mental image of thousands of feet marching north on this trail helped put him at ease despite the monumental task ahead.

The sun rode low in the eastern sky. Already blazing, Cesar knew the day would be long and brutal. He figured they had covered twenty-five or thirty kilometers since exiting the old Chevy on the Mexican side of the border. They were well inside the United States by now, far past the point of no return.

The going was slow. His ragtag group consisted of three men like himself, young, fit, and accustomed to working in the hot afternoon sun. However, unlike his first crossing, four women and two small children had also chosen to make the trip.

Cesar was prepared for the journey, had been for as long as he could remember. Ever since his deportation a year earlier following an Immigration and Customs Enforcement raid in Kansas City, he had focused every waking moment on preparations for his return. He had worked three jobs to raise enough cash to pay his *coyotero* and yet, he had fallen short. A five-hundred-dollar loan from his uncle had carried him over the top.

But the others? He knew little about whether they would survive the heat, the blistering pace, and the abject brutality of the Sonoran desert in the middle of the summer. He hoped so. He felt responsible for them, as if his previous experience north of the border had bestowed some sort of divine responsibility, an unseen burden he dared not abandon.

He took a sip of water and hitched up his jeans. At five-foot-four, with shoulder-length black hair tied in a loose ponytail, Cesar looked like a million other brown men toiling in the American service economy. His most distinguishing feature was his easy grin, an infectious, toothy smile that instantly put people at ease.

He started to spit, and then thought better of it, swallowing his saliva instead. *Need to conserve water out here,* he chastised himself. *Every drop counts…*

He took another step and kicked a rock to the side. His thoughts shifted to his family in Mexico. His mother, always overprotective of her youngest son, had gotten hysterical when he told her he was going north again. She had begged and pleaded with him, trying to convince him the Americans would put him in jail this time, lock him away for the rest of his life if he was caught.

His father, an unemployed mechanic, had taken a different approach. He understood the economic realities of Mexico; he saw firsthand the desperation of young men with nowhere to go, with nothing to do. He feared the lure of the drug cartels and realized it was only a matter of time before they swept his son into a life from which he would never return.

"The gringos love us when times are good," his father had said. "But if things are bad, like now, they will turn on you and make your life miserable. Don't ever forget that."

There was a rustling off to Cesar's right, on the other side of a patch of barrel cactus. *Conejo.* "Rabbit," Cesar whispered to himself, practicing his English.

He thought of his cousin Efrain. *Is he here? Is he lying feet from me, only bones, or did he make it? Maybe he was caught and is sitting in jail?* Efrain had left for Idaho three months earlier, but had never reached his destination. His disappearance, another sad example of the risks involved in going north, had been the talk of the town.

Cesar banished the thought from his mind and continued walking. A short, rock-covered hill rose in front of him. He started climbing. From the other side, below his line of sight, he heard shouting. Cocking his head, he tried to catch the words. It took him a moment to realize they were speaking English. What?

A crippling spike of fear tore through his gut as he crested the rise and got his first glimpse of the scene below. Two white men stood at the front of the line talking to Miguel, the *coyotero.* They carried menacing assault rifles and were dressed in desert camouflage from head to toe.

Cesar's first impression was *border patrol*, but upon closer inspection, he realized he was wrong. Neither man wore insignia on their uniform, nor did they have the close-shaved, professional look he associated with the patrol. Also, one was grossly obese, his belly tumbling over his belt like a sack of flour.

The fat man pointed at him. "You! Up there! Get down here!"

Cesar complied, picking his way carefully down the hill until he joined the rest of the group. As Cesar watched, the fat man barked at Miguel in staccato English, gesturing wildly with the barrel of his gun. His jowls shook like fresh jalea every time he moved his head.

Even more than the sun and the heat, Cesar feared bandits. But these men were something else—something new.

"What do you think is happening?" whispered the woman behind him. Cesar shrugged, trying to remain calm despite the ball of nausea percolating in his gut.

The fat man fired a short burst into the air. Everyone stopped talking. The woman moved closer, and her fingers sought out his arm. "*Tengo miedo*," she whispered. *I'm scared.*

"It's okay," Cesar lied.

The gunmen turned away and conversed in hushed tones, gesturing repeatedly at Cesar's terrified group and pointing north.

Cesar put his hand on the woman's shoulder. "Get ready to run." She shook her head vigorously and gestured at the other woman standing to the side with one of the children. "I can't. That's my sister and her daughter." Closing his eyes, Cesar said a quick prayer for the woman and her child.

He checked his rear, looking for other gunmen. It was clear. He visualized a canyon system they had passed a half-kilometer back where he could hide.

Miguel took a step forward, got in the slim gunman's face, and poked him in the chest. The man laughed and nudged his partner in the ribs. Cesar tensed, preparing for the worst. Faster than Cesar would have expected for a man his size, the fat man raised his rifle and leveled it at Miguel's face.

One of the children began to cry, calling for his father. Time slowed to a crawl. The gun against Miguel's head became his everything for an interminable instant, the bridge between the life and death. He couldn't tear his eyes away.

Crack! Miguel spun away and fell to the ground. A hawk cried out far above them.

"Does anyone else have a problem?" the shooter bellowed.

Cesar swallowed, his throat his own desert. As the murderer trained his gun on the remaining survivors, his partner kneeled beside Miguel's body and rolled it over. He rifled through the pockets until he found the dead man's wallet. Flipping it open, he pulled out a handful of pesos and American dollars and dropped them on the corpse's chest.

We're going to die now, Cesar realized with sudden clarity. *Right here. My family will never know what happened to me. Like Efrain.*

Behind him, the woman was praying, repeating the same bible verse. *"Padre me protege porque he pecado…"*

The man finished his search, and finding nothing of value, got to his feet. He whispered something to his partner.

With a wave of his gun, the fat man pointed at a towering saguaro. "Okay, everyone. By that cactus! Turn out your pockets!" The time to run had passed. Cesar had no choice but to comply. He cursed his cowardice and went to stand beside the cactus.

"On your knees!" the gunman screamed, his high-pitched voice sounding like one from a little girl on a playground. Cesar fell to his knees, closed his eyes, and tried to think about his family.

The men raised their weapons.

Seven

Taos, New Mexico

Jack realized Becka had reached the end of her patience when she hauled herself from the pit and plopped down in the grass. She stripped off her gloves, drew her knees up to her chin, and sighed.

"Okay, Bob Vila," she said with a tired grin. "If that's a fuel-oil tank, then tell me why it's buried in our front yard."

Jack shrugged and gazed at the ground between the house and the barrier, mentally tracing a long-dormant oil supply line to the furnace, which now ran on propane. "I guess that's how they did things—"

The phone rang, interrupting him

Jack scanned the yard, searching for the phone, then spied it on the front porch where he had left it earlier.

"I'll get it." He climbed to his feet. "I need to hit the bathroom anyway."

Grabbing the cordless phone from the top step, he answered the call.

"Jack! Oh, my God! I'm so glad I got you!" his mother cried from the receiver.

He straightened up, suddenly alert. *Something's wrong with the girls.* Before he could ask, she uttered the magic words, "Don't worry. Maddie and Ellie are fine."

Jack breathed a sigh of relief.

Her voice reedy with concern, his mother asked, "Have you seen the news this morning?"

"No. We've been—"

"Well, turn it on. Now." Jack's mother was not one to argue with. At sixty-four, and after raising six children, she knew what she wanted, and she didn't take no for an answer.

Jack made his way through the door and grabbed the remote. When he turned on the television, the flatscreen snapped to life, filling the room with the saccharine soundtrack from the girls' favorite cartoon series. He hit the mute button.

Ellie, he thought with a smile. Oldest by a minute and a half, Ellie had an all-consuming passion for everything on the Cartoon Network.

"Ok, Mom. The TV's on."

"Good. Now go to CNN."

Jack fumbled with the buttons, landing first on a gardening show. Cursing, he punched in the numbers again and was rewarded with the CNN logo. A thick red banner crawled across the bottom of the screen. The words 'Martial law declared,' printed in tall, bold, white letters, screamed for attention. *What the hell?* He cranked up the volume.

The camera cut to a long-distance shot. The commentator babbled frantically, talking over the remote reporter. Jack recognized Times Square. It looked nothing like he remembered. The camera swooped to street level.

Chaos. That was the only word he could think of to describe the events playing out on the screen. The streets seethed with people struggling with each other, dashing every which way. The faint *pop-pop-pop* of gunshots echoed somewhere off-camera.

He moved forward, trying to get a better view. Is that…? As if reading his mind, the camera panned and tightened on a man in a business suit sawing into the neck of a police officer who was lying in the middle of the street. Jack stared in fascinated disgust as two women joined the scene. One went for the officer's midsection, and the other latched onto an upper thigh. Blood arced through the air, and the man on the ground writhed in pain. Then he was still.

Jack gasped. "What's happening, Ma? Did someone attack New York again?"

She let out a low sob. "No… No one knows. Several hours ago, people started getting sick and attacking each other... It's everywhere. It's awful…"

Jack was incredulous. His heart pounded. He felt sick to his stomach. "That's impossible! Everywhere? Who…?"

"Yes. Everywhere. All over the world. Washington, London, Cairo…. everywhere."

He couldn't process what she was saying. "Hold on, Mom."

He went to the front door. "Becka! Something's going on. Come inside! Quick!"

As he returned his attention to the television, the live shot vanished, replaced by the scrolling *'Martial law declared'* message and a studio shot. A frazzled-looking young man, not an anchor Jack recognized, fiddled with his tie from his seat behind the main desk.

From off-camera, a staffer appeared and handed the anchorman a slip of paper before dashing back out of sight. The commentator scanned the note and frowned. He reached to his neck and loosened his tie, then wiped his brow. He seemed to age ten years in an instant.

"Ladies and gentlemen, I've just learned the president has declared Washington a complete loss. The government is evacuating." He gave a nervous cough and looked to one side. A million thoughts ran through Jack's mind. He had friends on the east coast, some in Washington. Becka touched his arm, and he jumped.

"Sorry," she said. "What's up?"

He gestured at the television. "There's something going on back east."

"It's everywhere!" his mother corrected. He had forgotten he was still on the phone.

Becka flipped over to MSNBC. Then Fox. The same story was playing on every channel.

Massive simultaneous attacks were occurring around the globe. People were turning on each other and acting like cannibals for no apparent reason.

"The kids!" Becka exclaimed, concern lining her face.

"Mom says they're fine." Jack took her hand.

"I'm scared." Becka said with her eyes still glued to the screen.

He returned his attention to the phone. "We'll be over in a few, Mom."

"Okay." She sounded distracted.

"What is it, Ma?"

She paused for a heartbeat, then answered, "There's someone at the door."

Jack's breath hitched in his throat. "Don't open it. Lock it and wait for us to get there," he ordered.

"I'll see you soon, dear," she replied. The line went dead.

Jack handed the phone to Becka and went to the kitchen to get his keys. She was still standing there, staring at the television, when he returned. He put his arm around her shoulder. "Becka, honey, we need to go now."

~~~

Five minutes later, he was banging on his mother's front door. "Ma! It's us! Let us in!"

The lock *snapped* loudly, and the door swung open. His mother motioned them through, slamming the door behind them and throwing the deadbolt once they were inside. "Did you see anything?" she asked, peering through the peephole.

Confused, Jack shook his head. "No. Everything looks normal."

"Is that your son?" a man's voice called out from the next room.
~~~

Jack's pulse quickened. "Who's that?"

His mother waved him off. "Don't worry. It's only Mr. Carhart, from next door. He can't get in touch with his family in Atlanta."

She ushered them into the living room where they found Mr. Carhart sitting in an easy chair nursing an enormous glass of scotch. He looked miserable.

"Where are the girls?" Becka asked immediately.

Jack's mom pointed at the ceiling. "Upstairs, napping."

"I'm going to go check on them." Becka looked at Jack with an obvious invitation to join her.

Jack hesitated, looked at his mom and then back at Becka. "I'll be right up."

"Okay," Becka said.

As Becka climbed out of sight, Jack turned to his mother. "Have you heard anything else about what's going on?"

She motioned towards the couch. "Yes. But you're going to want to sit for this…"

Eight

Boise, Idaho

Bump.

"Welcome to Boise, ladies and gentleman. The time here is ten forty-three AM. The temperature is seventy-eight degrees. We hope you enjoyed your flight and that you choose to fly with us again."

Huh?

"Please remain in your seat with your belts fastened until the aircraft comes to a complete stop."

Kevin Salerno opened his eyes and blinked.

His mouth was gummy and dry, as if someone had stuffed it with damp wool.

"You must've had a long trip," a voice on his right said. Kevin turned his head, following the sound. Sitting next to him was a middle-aged woman with big hair and a little too much makeup for her age. She held a paperback on her lap with her thumb tucked in to save her place. She looked like she was expecting an answer.

"Uh huh," he said noncommittally.

The plane was still rolling, but Kevin unbuckled his seatbelt anyway. His seatmate gave him a disapproving frown. The plane bumped to a stop, inched forward a few feet, then stopped again. The plane repeated the process twice more before they reached the gate. A chime sounded overhead, and all of the cabin lights flickered to life. The air conditioning kicked in, sending a stream of cool air against his forehead.

"Long trip," Kevin offered up to his nosy neighbor.

The woman smiled. "I'm going to see my grandkids. What about you?"

Kevin rolled his eyes. *Why do people always wait until landing to start talking? Can't they just leave well enough alone?* "Well, I hope you have a good visit," he said, ignoring her question and fiddling with his seatback.

She smiled, obviously believing he really gave a shit. "Me, too. Are you here for business or pleasure?"

"Neither," he said, offering no explanation.

She gave him a puzzled look.

"Look, Miss…"

"Martha." She smiled.

"Martha." He tried to force a smile, but failed. "I'm sorry, but I'm not very pleasant when I first wake up. I've had a really long week, and I just want to get home. I really hope you have a good time in town."

Martha's smile collapsed. "I just…"

"I know," Kevin said. "You just wanted to talk. Not today, though."

He turned his back on her, leaving her hanging mid-sentence, and stood to retrieve his carry-on from the luggage bin above. Starting in Shanghai the day before—or was it tomorrow? He always got confused—he had been on the move for twenty-two hours. This was the final leg of his trip. All that remained was an hour's drive home. He was so close he could taste it.

Ten rows forward, in what passed for Business Class in modern American air travel, the flight attendant disarmed the door. It popped open with a whoosh, and instantly the cool and humid ten-thousand-foot pressurized air he had been breathing since Seattle was replaced with the dry air of southern Idaho.

People began filing off of the airplane slowly at first, then picking up speed as they realized their brief period of captivity was finally over. As Kevin entered the jetway, he felt a deep sense of calm wash over his body. He had been on the road for the past two weeks negotiating a deal between his employer and a Shanghai component supplier. He was sick and tired of the road; he only wanted to be home with a beer in his hand and his feet propped up on the railing while he watched the sun set over the western mountains.

The line stopped moving. Passengers collided with each other, slow to react to the sudden stoppage. A chorus of groans echoed up the jet way. Kevin craned his head to see what was going on at the exit, but it was no use. There were too many people.

"Come on," he muttered. "Move your asses…" In his mind's eye, he could see his motorcycle waiting for him in the extended-stay parking lot. Another twenty minutes and he'd be roaring west to his cabin in the Boise foothills.

Someone screamed. A gun went off, the sound roaring through the confined space of the jetway like summer thunder. Kevin's insides turned to ice. He ducked down instinctively, trying to make himself a smaller target. A moment later, the flow of traffic reversed, and he found himself riding a panicked wave of humanity back toward the airplane.

Nine

High above Western Kansas

Captain Mike Pringle scratched his chin as he scanned the instrument cluster of the Boeing 757-200 that was hurtling west at four hundred and twenty knots. Everything checked out, as expected, and his thoughts drifted back to the previous evening.

Stuck in Washington because of severe thunderstorms, he had made the best of a bad situation, spending the night with an exotic Air France hostess named Barbara, who was also grounded by the weather. The sex had been phenomenal, lasting until dawn when he finally collapsed from sheer exhaustion. He had managed to squeeze in a few blissful hours of sleep, barely enough to meet the legal limit.

At forty-four, Mike was doing exactly what he wanted with his life. After a relatively successful career with the Air Force and two tours supporting the wars in Iraq and Afghanistan, he had opted for early retirement rather than chase the next set of bars on his shoulder. Life in the military meant long hours and low pay with the constant threat of people shooting at him. That was fine for the young guys, but he had bigger plans.

Since joining United Airlines three years earlier, he had methodically climbed the seniority ladder, to the point where he now spent most of his days high above the flyover states. The next step was to get on the international roster. He figured that was a year, maybe two, away. He didn't mind. Being a pilot had its perks, especially the steady supply of fresh new women.

He glanced at his copilot, Marty Sellers, and grinned. At fifty-one, the father of five, and a devout Mormon, Marty was the anti-Mike. Strangely enough, the men got along well, and they made a determined effort to work together whenever possible. Mike figured Marty enjoyed living through his exploits, getting a vicarious thrill at glimpsing a life he had forsaken.

"Big weekend plans?" Mike asked, looking to break the monotony of the trip.

Marty folded his novel over his knee and stretched. "Nothing major. Swim meets for my oldest."

It was Friday morning and they had a hundred and sixty-five people on a nonstop from DC to San Francisco. The flight was running a day late, but for the most part, the passengers weren't complaining. More storms were predicted for the weekend, and this was the only ticket out of town.

An amber light blazed into life on his console. Cabin call.

His radio squawked. "Sir? This is Brenda. We have a situation back here." Brenda was serving the rear. He hadn't worked with her before, but she had seemed professional enough during the preflight introductions. Mike raised an eyebrow at Marty.

"I'm listening…"

"A passenger in 36C. He's—"

Mike cut her off. "He's what?"

"He's having trouble breathing." A note of panic was creeping into her voice.

Mike relayed the information to Marty, and they exchanged a look of concern. There wasn't much either of them could do from the cockpit. FAA regulations barred them from leaving their seats to assist, even in the direst emergency.

"Hold on, Brenda. I'll find out if there's a doctor on board."

"Thank you."

Changing the radio to broadcast to the entire plane, Mike cleared his throat and put on his best voice of authority. "Ladies and gentlemen, we are experiencing a medical emergency. If there are any doctors or trained medical personnel on board, please press the call button located directly over your head. I repeat, if you are a doctor or you have medical training, press the flight attendant call button." He switched back to speak with Brenda. "Brenda?"

"Yes, Mike?"

"Any luck?"

"Yes, sir. Two passengers. JoAnne is collecting them." Good. JoAnne was in charge of the center of the plane. Mike had flown with her on several occasions and knew she had a solid head on her shoulders.

"Thanks. Keep me posted."

"Think it's serious?" Marty asked as Mike ended the call.

"Beats me. Can you check with ground control and let them know we may need to make an emergency landing?"

Marty nodded. "Sure. At this rate I don't think we're ever going to get home." He began murmuring into the radio. The plane was still a little over three hours from their final destination. If they had to put down early, it probably meant Denver or Salt Lake City.

Mike opened a line to Barbara again. "Barbara?"

She didn't respond at first, and then, suddenly, she screamed, an earsplitting howl of pain that drilled into Mike's brain. Mike tore his radio off and held it a few inches away, massaging his sore ears. "What was that?"

"Uh, Mike," Marty said tentatively. "Denver's not answering."

"Just a second Marty—" He dialed the volume down. "Barbara? What's going on?"

No response. Mike felt a tension headache building. He switched channels to first class. "I'm calling Chad." Chad was the senior flight attendant on board and should be near the phone. Mike relied upon his crew for a host of duties, not the least of which was security. There was no response. Maybe he's helping JoAnne, he ruminated, his concern mounting. He tried again. Three rings without an answer.

"Mike." Marty waved at him.

"What is it?"

"I can't raise Chicago, either..."

Mike was getting a bad feeling, the sort of tickle he had gotten in Afghanistan when a mission was about to go to shit. It wasn't something he could put his finger on, just an itch in the back of his mind, like bobbing on the ocean at night and feeling a large animal brushing against your legs.

Marty continued to fiddle with the communications system, switching frequencies, trying to raise the major air traffic control centers along their route, to no avail. "There must be someone else out there." He punched up a radar screen that displayed the airspace around them.

"Mike. Look!" He pointed at a blip ten miles out and closing. According to the transponder, the signal represented a Continental Airlines flight heading due east at twenty-six thousand feet.

Mike matched frequencies with the other airplane and keyed his transmitter. "Continental Eight Two, this is United Four One requesting ground relay." He held his breath as he waited for a response.

Finally, after what seemed like eternity, a female voice responded. "United Four One. This is Continental Eight Two. Negative on ground relay. Repeat. Negative on—" There was a sharp *BANG*, and the communications channel went silent.

"Continental Eight Two. United Four One. Come back."

Dead air.

As they watched, Continental 82 crossed through twenty thousand feet. Seventeen thousand. Ten thousand. It was going down.

The skies were clear, and Mike bent forward to the cockpit window, scanning for any trace of the other aircraft. It was difficult to see over the nose of the giant Boeing, but he thought he caught a flash of metal far below. He shared a solemn look with Marty. "I think they went down."

Marty double-checked the radar. Continental 82 had vanished.

Mike pulled out his mobile phone. *Three bars.* It was a long shot to place a call this high. The plane's speed relative to the towers on the ground would make holding a signal nearly impossible. "I'm gonna try headquarters," he said. "They'll be able to tell us what's happening."

Marty looked like he was in shock. Unlike Mike, he had no combat background. He had worked his way up to the right seat via the private aviation world, starting with small commuter aircraft hauling people up and down the West coast and eventually graduating to the big jets.

Mike dialed the switchboard in Chicago and pressed *Send.* The line rang three times before he was connected. A voicemail recording came on with a stock message explaining that the navigation menu had recently changed and recommending he listen closely to ensure he reached the correct party.

Mike cursed, and praying for an operator, mashed down on the zero button. He needed someone who could tell him what the hell was going on.

Crash!

That was in first class, Mike thought. It sounded like a drink cart tipping over.

He pulled the phone away from his ear and motioned to Marty. The door had a sliding security peephole mounted at eye-level, a means of inspecting the length of the cabin without exposing themselves to anyone trying to take control of the aircraft.

Before Marty could respond, the cockpit door rattled with a direct impact. But it held. Visions of Continental 82 flashed through Mike's head as he speculated on what was happening in the rear. Thoughts of 9/11 intermingled with his fear. *Are we under attack again?*

For the first time, Mike was grateful for the reinforced doors. He had bitterly opposed their introduction when they had first been announced. He felt that as a pilot he had a responsibility to show his face to the crew and passengers and to be accessible at all times.

Putting his phone up to his ear, he motioned for Marty to check the door. Marty unfastened his harness and made his way between the seats to the peephole. Sliding the cover aside, he put his eye to the door. There was another impact, and Marty jerked reflexively.

"What is it?" Mike asked, curiosity burning a hole in his gut.

"Hold on." Marty tried again. Mike watched with anticipation. Meanwhile, the phone continued to ring. Marty took a quick step back, his face ashen. "This is not happening…"

Ashen faced, he returned to his seat.

"Marty?" Mike said. "What's happening back there? Tell me, damn it!"

Marty's answer was a rapid shake of his head. His eyes were bugged out, and he looked like he was about to be sick. Mike sighed, placed his cell phone on the console, and climbed out of the pilot's chair. He approached the peephole cautiously, keeping one eye on Marty.

Mike's brain refused to process the sight on the other side of the door. He froze, unable to comprehend the atrocity playing out feet from where he stood.

A man was lying on the floor with Chad hunched over him ripping and tearing at the man's throat like a starving lion on the Serengeti. Greasy bits of flesh and gristle dangled from Chad's teeth. Splatters of blood coated the cabin, staining the walls a dark red, congealing on the floor in viscous puddles of liquid gore.

A knot of passengers huddled farther back in the center aisle. As Mike prepared to turn away, a ruined face popped up inches from his own on the other side of the door. It mashed against the peephole, blocking his view. Mike held his breath and forced himself to remain still. The figure moved away from the peephole, leaving Mike with a view of the cabin blurred by some unidentifiable bodily fluid. A moment later, the figure charged the door, the force of the impact bending the door in its frame, showing cracks of light from the cabin around the edges.

Mike flailed away from the door.

"What the hell was that?" Marty asked.

"He knows we're here," Mike replied, shaking uncontrollably. He sank into his seat and buckled in the safety harness. He had to think, had to land the plane.

"Mike?" Marty asked again.

"I don't know what's going on," Mike snapped. "But we need to get on the ground now." Pulling on his headset, he began skipping through the radio frequencies, frantically searching for someone, anyone, to guide them in.

Ten

A warm wind pressed at Cesar's back; sand tickled his back where his shirt had ridden up.

Someone coughed. *"Senõr,"* a woman hissed. "They're gone."

Cesar opened his eyes and stole a glance over his shoulder, bracing himself for the shot that was sure would come. They were gone. "What…?"

She shook her head as if to say she had no idea. "Look!" She frowned and pointed in the opposite direction. Cesar's eyes followed her outstretched hand. Ten or twenty meters away, on the far side of a narrow arroyo, a lone figure stumbled through the desert.

Cesar struggled to his feet, his knees popping in protest. He scanned his surroundings to be sure the gunmen were truly gone. When he saw no traces of them, he relaxed and turned his attention to the newcomer, whom he now saw was a man.

Something bothered him about the way the man moved. He looked *stiff;* his steps were forced, as if he wasn't in control of his own muscles. *Maybe he's delirious? Out of water?*

Cesar cringed as the man plowed into a monstrous cholla cactus at full speed, inch-long needles plunging into his body, impaling him a thousand times over. The stranger began a silent struggle with his thorny adversary, twisting and jerking, trying to pull himself loose. Finally, he pulled free and resumed his solitary march, ropy cholla segments trailing in his wake.

"Madre de dios," Cesar said. "Did you see that?" He waved at the man. *"Hola! Senõr!"*

Like a fast-moving school of fish, the stranger shifted course, vectoring toward the sound of Cesar's voice.

"Watch out!" Cesar yelled as the man approached the edge of the arroyo. He cursed. *Is he blind?* Without a word, the man stepped over the brink and tumbled out of sight.

"We need to help him," Cesar said, taking off at a run. The others followed.

The soil at the edge was loose and crumbly, shot through with deep furrows from recent rains. There was no sign of the stranger.

"Where did he go?" one of the women asked. "I don't see him…"

"Down there!" a man to Cesar's right shouted, pointing at a sharp bend where the creek jogged south. "I think he went that way."

Cesar squinted. "Wait. What's that?" There was a something wedged in the rocks at the base of the far wall. "We need to get down there," Cesar announced. "He might be hurt." He looked at the others, hoping someone would accompany him. When no one volunteered, he set off by himself.

The first thing he noticed was the smell. Like meat left in the sun, it permeated the air at the bottom of the wash. He picked his way through a nest of sun-bleached saguaro skeletons and grasped for the object. The smell was worse here. Tucking his nose into his shoulder, he wrapped his fingers around the end and tugged. The object popped loose. It took a second for his mind to comprehend what he held in his hands: A human arm, brown and desiccated, skin worn away in patches, yellow-white bone showing through. With a shocked yelp, Cesar dropped the arm and took a step back.

There was a commotion above. A thin stream of dirt trickled onto his shoulder. He glanced up. All faces were focused south, fixated on something he couldn't see.

"Get out!" one of the men yelled. "He's coming back!"

Out of the corner of his eye, Cesar saw the arm convulse. Before he could react, the hand latched onto his ankle with a viselike grip and started to squeeze. Cesar screamed and kicked out, trying to dislodge the arm, but it wouldn't release its grip.

"Hurry," came the call from above. The wind picked up, pushing up from the south. Cesar gagged at the stench. It was the same smell of putrefied rot attached to his leg, only worse. And it was coming toward him.

He heard the man before he saw him. Grunting and wheezing, what he assumed was the former owner of the arm rounded the bend and lumbered towards Cesar. His remaining arm was outstretched in a sick parody of pleading.

The pressure on Cesar's ankle eased for a second as the hand scuttled up his leg like an enormous spider. When it reached his calf, it clamped down again, digging bony fingertips into the soft flesh and muscle, triggering a spike of pain that shot through his body. His vision dimmed and he staggered against the wall of the arroyo, barely catching himself on a protruding root. The pain was unlike anything he had ever experienced. He beat at the hand, but that only made it worse. Filthy, broken fingernails dug into the denim of his jeans, scrabbling for bare skin.

Pebbles clattered. Branches snapped. He looked up and saw the man was less than five yards away. Seeing him up close, Cesar finally understood how much trouble he was in. The man was sick. His face was shredded to the bone. Mottled clumps of something sticky covered his scalp. His eyes, what was left of them, were an opaque gray, the color of monsoon storm clouds, filled with thick cataracts.

Setting off with a limp, Cesar headed for a narrow trail leading to the rim. As he ran, the attached hand leaped higher, fingers encircling his knee, squeezing the twin tendons on the back of his leg, making it all but useless.

"Help me!" he cried, frantically searching for the other border crossers. He was halfway up the slope when he finally succumbed to the pain, unable to go any farther.

A furtive glance over his shoulder revealed his pursuer, not far behind, still struggling with the incline.

Cesar dug into his pocket and withdrew his knife. He flipped the blade open. Taking care not to cut himself, he slid it between the hand and his leg and twisted. The knife sank into the desiccated flesh. There was no blood. The grip increased and a sudden bolt of pain lanced down to his foot. He bit back a cry and kept digging.

Finally, with a dry *crack*, the thumb broke away. The hand tumbled away from his leg and slid down the embankment, disappearing over a ledge.

Cesar wiped the knife blade in the sand, checked his leg, and finding no open wounds, continued his mad dash towards safety.

Eleven

Colorado Springs

Peter Woo flipped open the lid of his laptop and drummed his fingers on the palm rest, barely able to contain his excitement. He glanced at his mobile phone lying on the couch beside his thigh, and then turned his attention back to the laptop as his screen flashed.

At seventeen, Peter felt he had a pretty good idea how the world worked; God had a plan, and if you followed it, you were golden. If you ignored it, you were on the express train to Hell. Peter was following the plan to the letter, as delivered by Pastor Chuck at Central Baptist Community Church, and he felt little sympathy for anyone who wasn't doing the same.

After what seemed like an eternity, the laptop finally booted. He swiped his fingertip on the scanner, logging himself in. A few seconds later, he was on Facebook, skipping through his news feed.

Peter was intimately familiar with the idea of Rapture—how, when mankind faced its final battle, Jesus would return to the earth and carry the true believers to Heaven to sit by his side.

That was why he was so excited. His wall told the entire story. The rapture was here...

.

.

.

Johnny Gaston
I just saw a non-believer taken down in the street! Stay strong, everyone!
8 minutes ago - Like this

Emily Felt
He is arrived! Praying!
7 minutes ago
Jessica Fox likes this

Johnny Gaston
There's someone at the door… brb
6 minutes ago - Like this

Emily Felt
Who was it Johnny?
6 minutes ago - Like this

Emily Felt
Johnny? Are you there? Who was it?
4 minutes ago - Like this

Chris Neelon
Emily - where are you?
3 minutes ago - Like this

Emily Felt
Johnny? Call me, k? Praying for you.
1 minute ago

.

.

.

Peter had to admit, as happy as he was about the rapture, he was scared for his family, for his girlfriend. *For himself.* Pastor Chuck hadn't said anything about people eating each other. Come to think of it, he hadn't seen the pastor on Facebook all day. That was odd. The Pastor was a regular on Facebook, always there to offer a guiding hand.

Peter shrugged. *He's probably busy helping people rapture.* He recalled his recent phone call with Molly, his girlfriend of eight months. She had called twenty minutes earlier, crying, saying she had heard gunshots outside her house. Things seemed worse on her end of town, the rapture in full swing. Peter wished he was there with her so they could experience it together. And he would be if it weren't for his mother. He turned his eyes to the ceiling. She lay just a few feet above, suffering from the end stages of terminal ovarian cancer. He and his father had brought her home from the hospital the week before. Her last round of chemotherapy was a complete disaster, draining her strength and turning her into a ghost of the woman who once ruled the house with an iron fist. The end was close, he knew. He couldn't help but smile at the timing. Soon he would see his mom in Heaven; she would be strong and healthy like he remembered.

Peter thought it was strange that his dad hadn't called yet. He picked up his cell phone and checked the time. Two twenty. *He said he'd be home by now.* He shrugged it off. His father would get home when he did.

He typed in a quick Facebook post, encouraging his friends to 'hold tight in the name of Jesus. The end is near!'

As he pressed enter, his phone chirped. It was Molly. He picked it up. "Hey."

"Pete." She was crying and gasping, almost hyperventilating.

"What is it? Are you okay?"

She blubbered something he couldn't understand. Something about eating… He slid off the couch and went to the window. When he peered out, he saw nothing but empty street.

"Slow down, Molly," he said, motioning with his hand even though she couldn't see it.

She blew her nose loudly in his ear. "They ate them," she spit out. "The police—all of them."

Peter was confused. "What do you mean *they ate them?* What did the police eat?"

"No, Pete!" she shrieked. "The people outside! They ate the police that were shooting at them." Peter closed his eyes and tilted his head toward the ceiling. She was panicking again.

"I don't understand what you're saying, Molly. Try to slow down and start from the beginning."

She did, and when she was finished, Peter realized he couldn't wait any longer for his father to get home. If he really loved Molly, he had to go to her right now, to be with her for the end. He checked the street again. *Still nothing.* His family home was situated in the center of a cul-de-sac, and the closest main road was a half-mile away. Everything looked normal.

He went back to the couch and pulled his computer back into his lap. After entering the address of the local news station in his browser, he clicked on their live traffic cameras. The page finally loaded, displaying a blue screen—a dead video feed.

"Hold on, Molly." He picked up the remote, turned on the television, and switched it to the same news channel.

A young blonde woman at the anchor desk had her hand up to her ear, her head tilted as she listened to a personal earphone. She was frowning. As he watched, her frown deepened, the corners of her mouth turning her pretty face ugly. She straightened up, rearranged the papers on her desk, and locked her eyes on the camera.

"According to national sources, the president has declared martial law in all fifty states. A twenty-four-hour curfew has been imposed. The Army and National Guard have been mobilized and have orders to shoot anyone violating this curfew." The anchor shook uncontrollably as she spoke, looking as if she were about to start crying.

"Ladies and gentlemen, my… our advice remains the same. Stay in your homes with your doors and windows locked. There is some form of contagion spreading throughout the country. It causes extreme confusion and violence in those affected, and they are no longer safe to be around. I repeat. Stay indoors. Lock your doors and windows. Do not answer the door for anyone."

"Molly?"

"Are you coming?" She was crying again.

"Yes." Peter swallowed. "I'll be there as soon as I can."

The anchor woman stood, unclipped her microphone and tossed it on the desk, and then walked off-camera. Peter snapped his laptop shut and stuffed it in his courier bag. There was one last thing to do before he left. He dashed up the carpeted stairs two at a time and raced down the hall to his parents' room. The door was closed, but he heard the muted sounds of their television on the other side. He rapped on the door with the back of his hand.

"Mom?"

There was no response. Peter hesitated, then knocked again, louder this time. "Mom? Can I come in?"

There was still no answer. That presented a dilemma. She often dozed during the day, when the pain wasn't too bad. But once, several weeks before, he had entered her room to find her half-naked, hugging the toilet in the master bathroom. He blushed at the memory. The sense of embarrassment at seeing his mother's naked body had almost made him turn and run. But instead, he had bent down and helped her up. But he couldn't forget the sight.

He turned the door knob and pushed in with his shoulder, while trying to keep his eyes glued to the floor. Glancing up carefully, he saw that the bed was empty, the sheets twisted into a ball. No. Not again. His spirits sank. Peter pushed the door the rest of the way open and stepped into the room. He wrinkled his nose. What's that smell? It was like something rotting, like an old styrofoam meat tray in the kitchen trash he had forgotten to take out.

He went to the bathroom door. It was closed, but he could see light underneath. "Mom! Are you okay?"

That's a stupid question, he realized as soon as it crossed his lips. Of course she's not okay.

"Mom?" He knocked.

Crash!

The door rattled in its frame. A chunk of hollow core laminate fell to Peter's feet. A crack as long as his arm appeared in the top panel. Peter stepped back, wringing his hands. The smell was stronger now. There was another impact, followed by a mad scrabbling on the other side, as if a dog were trapped inside, trying to dig its way through. Peter took a tentative step forward and placed his ear a few inches from the door.

"I'm opening the door now, Mom." He put his hand on the knob. A guttural moan emanated from the bathroom, deep and long like an old tornado siren. He twisted the knob slowly, trying to guess when the latch would cross the strike plate. Just when he thought it was almost there, the door was wrenched from his hand. His finger caught on the head of a screw in the knob, ripping a deep furrow along the length. Blood poured from his hand.

Peter gasped at the sight before him.

His mother stood hunched and naked in the doorway. The shriveled remains of her breasts swayed like rotten pears; the bones of her hips flared out in bold relief, rigid wings stretching her gray, mottled skin like a bizarre tent made of human flesh. Clotted blood coated her thighs. Something writhed between her legs, something small yet very alive, something that had clawed its way from inside her body.

Peter squeaked in fear. She rushed at him, a feral hunger on her face, focused on her next meal. *Just like the people on television,* he thought absently. He turned and ran for his life.

Twelve

Megan burst from her trailer at full speed. Her eyes were wild as she searched for someone, anyone, who could help her with Sam. The nearest trailer was twenty feet away, diagonal from hers. She sprinted across the baked dirt and tugged on the cheap aluminum door. *Locked.* The adjacent trailer was the same.

She stood in the hot sun and racked her brain, trying to remember who was working today, and who was off. *Katy's on*, she recalled. *She said so at dinner last night.* A lithesome, African-American woman from Miami, Katy was Megan's closest friend in the brothel. For reasons Megan still didn't understand, they had become quick friends when she first arrived, often watching television together between shifts, doing each other's hair, and even taking shopping trips into Las Vegas.

Megan set off at a dead sprint for the brothel, a five-thousand-square-foot, 1960s-era, ranch-style house . It lay just behind the next trailer.

"Help!" she screamed, as she burst through the rear door. "I need help!" There was no answer. Her pulse boomed in her ears, blotting everything else out. *Wait...* She heard the television in the ready room, three doors down. Megan raced down the hall, skidding to a stop on the scuffed laminate floor just outside the room where the girls on duty waited to be called for their lineup. Katy and another girl, Melissa, were perched on the edge of a dusty leather sofa. Their eyes were glued to the television.

Megan couldn't help but look. The screen was divided into four quadrants. The top left displayed an empty news anchor desk while the other three showed remote camera views of various city streets. Wandering aimlessly, figures lurched across the screen. Signs of destruction abounded. Cars sat with their doors open, dead bodies littered the streets, fires blazed in the distance.

Katy tore her gaze from the television. "Megan!" she exclaimed.

Megan gulped like a fish, trying to catch her breath. "I need help! Sam's in trouble! In my trailer!"

"Have you seen this?" Melissa asked, gesturing at the screen.

Megan nodded. "Yeah, but that's not important right now. Something's wrong with Sam!"

Katy unfolded herself from the couch and crossed the room while keeping one eye on the television the entire way. Megan felt like she was about to scream. *What the hell is going on here?*

"I'm sorry, Megs," Katy said, finally tearing her attention from the screen. "What's wrong with her?"

Leaving Melissa behind, Megan grabbed Katy's hand and yanked her down the hall and out the back door.

She filled Katy in as they ran to her trailer. "We were talking, and she just collapsed. I - I couldn't find a pulse…I tried…" The trailer door was wide open, swinging in a soft breeze.

As soon as they stepped inside, Megan was assaulted by a fetid tsunami of human shit and rancid body odors. It triggered her gag reflex, almost making her throw up.

"Ew! What is that smell?" Katy asked, holding her nose.

Megan gagged again and put her hand over her mouth. "I don't know." Sam was gone.

"She was right there," Megan insisted, pointing at the floor. "I swear!"

Katy poked her head into the small bathroom. "She's not in here either."

A horrible image flashed through Megan's mind: Sam struggling to her feet, leaving the trailer, wandering into the desert, and dying under the blistering sun. She felt sick. She should have stayed with her.

Someone outside screamed. It went on and on, making the hairs on the back of her neck stand on end.

"What was that?" Megan whispered. Katy shrugged, wide-eyed. They abandoned the stench to race outside and back to the brothel.

Megan tore the back door of the brothel open and pushed inside with Katy in tow. She called out, "Melissa? Are you okay?" Then she listened.

A wave of relief coursed through her as she recognized Sam's form at the far end of the hall, outside the television room. *She must have gone around to the front…*

Megan's relief was shattered a moment later as her eyes finally adjusted to the gloomy interior. Sam, who only minutes before had been lying on her trailer floor with no pulse, was hunched over Melissa, tearing chunks of flesh from her face and wolfing them down like a starving mutt. Melissa fought for her life, pummeling Sam, trying to dislodge her. Blood coated the hallway, enormous abstract splashes on both walls and a pool fanning out on the laminate floor. The house smelled of copper and feces.

Sam growled and tore a chunk from Melissa's neck. A high-pressure stream of arterial blood spurted forth, coating Sam's face, seeming to drive her into an even greater frenzy. Melissa stopped struggling and went limp. Katy screamed, and Sam's head snapped in their direction. *Shit!*

Pressing down on Melissa's corpse for leverage, Sam struggled to her feet. She moaned, and a thick chunk of Melissa's neck escaped her mouth and tumbled to the floor with a juicy *plop*. Her tongue skittered over her lips licking hungrily at the torrent of gore cascading from her open maw.

She started walking toward Megan and Katy. Quickly gaining speed, Sam charged down the shotgun-style hall with her bare feet slapping wildly. Megan was frozen in place. She felt like she was watching an instant replay on television. Sam's eyes bored into her with an inhuman determination. She had to move. *Right now.*

Fingers wrapped around her wrist. It was Katy, tugging her back through the door. Out of the corner of her eye, she saw something that shook her to her very core: Melissa rolling over, climbing to her feet. She spun on her heels and followed in a blind panic.

"Close the door!" Katy yelled once they were outside. Megan turned around and yanked the door shut. They raced back across the graveled area that passed for her front yard. Inside her trailer, Megan slammed the door closed behind them and set the deadbolt with a *clunk*.

"Oh, my God. Oh, my God. This isn't happening!" Katy sobbed, pacing around the trailer.

Megan went to the window and pulled the curtain back. "Oh, shit!" She dropped the curtain. "Here she comes!"

Katy stood in the middle of the room hugging herself and quaking. The window in the center of the door shattered, sending shards of glass spraying across the room. A pair of arms plunged through the window, waving around, seeking purchase. Sam roared in frustration.

Megan looked at Katy. "We have to go." Katy didn't argue. Grabbing her purse, Megan turned it upside down and dumped it on the bed. "Keys…" Her cell phone, a lipstick, and a pack of cigarettes left over from a long weekend in Vegas tumbled out. And then she spotted her keys.

She snatched them from the bed, but her hands were shaking so badly she almost dropped them.

"How?" Katy asked.

Megan pointed toward the other end of the trailer. "The bathroom window. My car's right outside."

"What if they…?"

The door shook and bulged with a brutal impact. The lock wouldn't hold much longer.

Megan shook her head emphatically and gestured at the front door. "We don't have a choice."

"Okay."

The girls squeezed into the tiny bathroom and slid the thin pocket-door closed. It would offer even less of a barrier than the front door, a few seconds at most. As Megan twisted the thumb-lock, the front door exploded open, and Sam roared. *She's inside*! Her insides turned into water.

She raised the bathroom window and stuck her head out. There was no sign of Melissa... yet. Climbing onto the toilet, she began to shimmy through the gap, gouging her ribcage on the sill in the process. With a final push, she tumbled out and landed on the ground beside her car.

She leaped to her feet and reached up, ready to help Katy.

It was too late. Katy was halfway through the window when she was yanked back with a scream. Megan shrieked. "Katy!"

She hopped in the air, trying to see through the window, but it was no use. She was too short. She searched for something to stand on, but couldn't find anything.

From inside the trailer, she heard muffled cries from Katy as Sam was probably tearing her limb from limb. The crying stopped a moment later, replaced by a sound that reminded her of her childhood dog—a Great Dane named Max—when he ate wet dog food.

"Katy! Come on, Katy."

Sam appeared at the window with a maniacal smile plastered across her face. When she leaned out, blood dripped from her face and hands down the side of the trailer. She started to wriggle her blood-soaked torso through the window.

Katy was dead, Megan realized. She dashed for her car. Her fire-red Volkswagen Electric was her pride and joy, purchased after a particularly busy month last year. She dropped her keys on the floor twice before she got it started. For a terrifying moment, she thought it wasn't working. Then she saw the light on the dash. In her rearview mirror, she saw Sam tumble to the ground behind her.

Megan didn't wait to find out what would happen next. Throwing the car into drive, she mashed down on the accelerator and shot off in a spray of gravel.

Thirteen

Somewhere in the Pacific Ocean

United States Navy Commander Betty Hollister accepted a Diet Coke from her warrant officer and turned her attention back to her display. At thirty-nine years old, she was the first woman in her family to make it out of her ancestral home in Mobile, Alabama, and the first woman to ever command a ballistic nuclear missile submarine for the Navy.

The USS Wyoming had been steaming north-northwest for seven days since leaving their new home base of Pearl Harbor, and they were making good time. All mission parameters were within acceptable ranges except for an intermittent vibration in the screw at eleven knots. If all went according to schedule, the sub would arrive at its duty station in the Bering Sea in the next forty-eight hours. The plan was to patrol for thirty days before moving on to their next duty station, the location of which had yet to be revealed. Commander Hollister took a sip of her drink and placed it in the gimbaled holder beside her right hand. The drink holder was designed to allow her drink to remain level as the sub moved around it.

Life as the first female commander of a boomer exceeded her wildest expectations. When she had first put in her papers to transfer from the carrier service to the submarine forces, her commanding officer, a grizzled veteran of the first Gulf War had given her a quizzical look and raised an eyebrow. "You know the trailblazer takes all the arrows, don't you?"

Her response had been simple. "I don't have a choice, sir." The Navy was all she knew, and like every other aspect of her life, she found she could only move forward, taking on ever-increasing responsibility in an unrelenting quest to remake herself, to leave her past behind.

Hollister's initial enlistment in the Navy had been a calculated move to avoid suspicion related to the accidental death of a classmate during her senior year of high school.

Only she knew the death was not accidental. Far from it. It had all started the summer between her junior and senior years when her best friend since elementary school, Susan Crawford, had stolen her boyfriend, humiliating her and destroying what had seemed like the perfect relationship with the perfect boy. Hollister was devastated, unable to accept the betrayal. Something shifted deep inside of her, some fundamental piece of her psyche she neither understood nor controlled. With a resolve and cunning that would serve her well in her future naval career, she suppressed her rage and acted as if she accepted the betrayal, even going so far as to offer her congratulations to the new couple, assuring them she bore them no ill will. And then, she waited. Four months later, on the night of homecoming, she made her move.

Shortly after midnight at a post-game party at a classmate's house, Hollister discovered her ex-boyfriend passed out cold in an overstuffed La-Z-Boy.

Hollister didn't hesitate. She was alone with him, and she knew Susan was at the other end of the house doing tequila shots with a group of girls from her field hockey team. Pinching his nose closed, Hollister cupped her hand over his mouth and counted to a hundred. The boy barely struggled, throwing out only a few halfhearted kicks as his autonomous nervous system reacted belatedly to the dwindling supply of oxygen. But it was too little, too late.

If I can't have you, then neither can she.

After verifying he was dead, Hollister slipped from the room and returned to the party. She stayed for another half-hour, acting as if nothing had happened, before slipping out and returning home.

Word spread quickly about the death at the party, and while the official cause of death was ruled an accidental asphyxiation, Betty was able to sleep through the night for the first time in months, finally satisfied justice had been served.

She had enlisted in the Navy the next day. After her first tour of duty, she applied to the Naval Academy, and from that point on, her career took off like a rocket.

Her transfer was official two months after graduation from the Naval Academy. She became the first female executive officer, or XO, serving aboard the USS New Mexico—the only female among an all-male crew. The first few weeks at sea had been brutal, but the crew eventually adjusted to the new reality as she demonstrated her competency as a senior officer. It didn't hurt that she ruled with an iron fist. Two years later, she had gotten her chance to command the Wyoming.

The Wyoming was loaded with a full complement of twenty-four Trident II D-5 missiles, each carrying eight W88 warheads rated at four hundred and seventy-five kilotons, for a total of over ninety-one megatons of firepower, or over seven thousand times the explosive force unleashed on Hiroshima. It was an awesome responsibility, one Commander Hollister did not take lightly.

She focused on her screen, tabbing through a diagnostic program containing information ranging from water pressure on the double-walled titanium hull down to the status of individual valves and sensors scattered throughout the leviathan. The software was a recent upgrade to the Ohio-class boats, and the Wyoming was the first to employ it in a live setting. So far, Hollister was impressed.

She changed screens to a crew roster and traced a finger down the list of names, reciting them to herself. Her crew was top notch, her executive team hand-picked. She trusted them with her life as they did with theirs. Yawning, she checked the time. There were only two more hours in her shift.

The Navy operated on an eight-hour day while at sea. That practice made some things easier for the people at the bottom of the food chain, but it made life a nightmare for the commander. Although her shift was almost over, she was never really off duty.

"Commander, we have an EAM," her chief communications officer announced. Tapping and swiping her screen, Hollister pulled the message from the submarine's central computer to her personal workspace.

"Acknowledged."

She tried to remember if there was a launch exercise scheduled for today. They occurred periodically during every tour as a tried-and-true means of ensuring the crew was prepared for action. She opened her personal calendar to check and didn't see anything. *Why the Emergency Action Message then?*

She paged her executive officer, Lieutenant Andrew Pollard, and began to read.

EAM: 1015Z. IMMEDIATE STRATEGIC WEAPON RELEASE AUTHORIZED. TARGET PACKAGE XT-234. AUTHORIZATION YTB778BAC.

Hollister sucked in her breath and reread the message. Emergency action messages were short by nature. The system relied upon a miles-long antenna array towed behind the submarine collecting ultra low frequency radio transmissions from enormous land-based radios scattered across the globe. EAMs were wrapped in several layers of encryption and unreadable by anyone other than herself.

She leaned back in her chair and surveyed the bridge crew. She opened a window on her console and pulled up a list of target packages. Hollister didn't recognize the 'X' designator in the targeting package and, as far as she knew, there were no conflicts in the world that could possibly warrant a strategic nuclear response of the magnitude specified in the EAM. Confused, she rubbed her temples.

The target package database appeared, and she paged through the list searching for X-234. When she reached the bottom of the page and didn't find it, she scrolled back to the top, double-checking in case she had missed it. On the right side of the screen was a slowly pulsing link marked *FCON*. She scratched her head. She had never noticed it before, despite endless hours on the simulator. She clicked the link and the screen flashed once, and was then replaced with two boxes. The first requested her command authorization code, and the second asked for a mission profile.

"What the hell?"

The command authorization code was a secret string of digits assigned to each officer possessing nuclear weapon release authority. The code served as one half of a key, the other half being provided with the EAM launch profile.

She punched in her code, along with the mission profile, XT-234. The screen flashed red, and the boxes appeared again, empty, but shaded a bright orange. Entering through the forward hatch, her XO finally arrived on the bridge. He came to her side, making a point of not looking directly at her display. He had served with her as far back as her carrier days and was her most trusted advisor.

Biting her lip, Hollister plugged in the command authorization code and the mission profile, and then she pressed Enter.

She gasped in surprise. The screen displayed twenty-four XT-level targeting packages. But it wasn't the number of packages that alarmed her, it was the targets.

The first entry, XT-102, covered Western and Southern Europe. The next entry, XT-118, had targets in South America—Lima, Rio de Janeiro, São Paolo—as did the next several profiles. She continued scrolling, looking for XT-234. It was at the bottom.

Seattle
Los Angeles
San Francisco
Sacramento
Las Vegas
Boise
Phoenix
Honolulu
Portland

The list went on and on. She blinked several times to ensure she wasn't seeing things. *Honolulu. That's Home.*

Hollister slid from her chair and motioned for Pollard to follow her. "Come with me," she said. "We need to talk."

"Commander?" Pollard asked once they were in her quarters. Hollister didn't reply. Instead, she went to her sea locker and rummaged around for a moment before pulling out a full bottle of Glenmorangie scotch and two plastic tumblers. Technically, alcohol wasn't allowed on Navy vessels. But as commander, she had the authority to bend the rules when she saw fit. And this situation called for a lot of bending. She splashed two fingers into each cup, and then added another. Shoving one toward Pollard, she motioned for him to drink up.

"Is it the EAM?" he asked.

She sighed and cast her eyes at the floor as she drained her scotch. It burned going down, and she felt a familiar ball of warmth blossom in her gut.

She snapped back. "Yes, Andrew. It is about the goddamned EAM."

"May I ask what is said?"

She nodded. "Full strategic launch. Target package XT-234."

Pollard gave her a puzzled look. "I'm not familiar with that package."

"Neither was I." She went to her terminal and rerouted the display from the bridge. When the list filled her screen, she spun the display around so Pollard could see. Bending in close, he recited each name under his breath as he worked his way to the bottom.

He sucked in his breath and looked up at Hollister when he finished reading. "Holy mother of God! Is this for real?"

She shrugged. "I assume so. I'm not aware of a countermand EAM."

Pollard drained the remains of his scotch in one gulp and held out his cup for a refill.

Hollister poured for both of them. "I don't know about you, Andrew, but this violates every oath I've ever taken. This is insane." He looked thoughtful for a moment as he evaluated her statement, then took a sip of his scotch. Hollister knew that by questioning the validity of the targeting package, she was offering him an opening to question her authority and possibly judge her unfit for duty. However, the expression on Pollard's face and his body language told her that he was just as shocked as she was.

Straightening in his chair, he broke his silence. "I recommend we proceed to periscope depth and attempt direct communication with Pearl."

Hollister hid her relief. "I concur. Send the order."

Pollard began entering commands for the bridge while Hollister got up and stalked around the tiny cabin, inspecting, but not seeing the numerous commendations arrayed on the bulkhead. She sensed an abrupt tilt in the deck as the officer at the helm implemented Andrew's request.

Together, they watched as the depth display on her computer rolled backward with agonizing slowness. Neither said a word, each lost in their own thoughts.

As they approached the surface, Hollister began to tense. She was breaking protocol by ignoring the EAM and surfacing in the open ocean. But she felt she had no choice. She had to know why she was being instructed to launch against the United States. They reached their target depth a minute later, and a hidden series of jets and pumps automatically adjusted the ballast, locking them in place.

Pollard bypassed the radio room and accessed the secure ship-to-shore communications subsystem. This mechanism was much more effective than the Ultra Low Frequency transmission by which they had received the EAM, allowing instantaneous communications either by satellite or direct line-of-sight broadcast to the shore.

"Calling Pearl," he said, as he pressed the connect icon on the screen. They waited. Hollister started to get a bad feeling. This was highly unusual.

"Try San Diego," she said after a few seconds, fear percolating inside. Pollard's fingers flew over the keyboard as he rerouted their request. San Diego was quiet as well.

They spent the next several minutes running through the various contact points in their chain of command before straying outside, first to the other naval vessels, and then to other branches of the armed forces, all to no avail. The military nets were silent.

"Do you know how to tap into the commercial infrastructure?" Hollister asked, frustrated. She knew it was possible, but she had never done it.

"Maybe," Pollard replied thoughtfully.

"Do it."

"We should be close enough to Russia to pick up terrestrial digital broadcasts. And we should be able to tap into some commercial satellites as well, pick up international traffic," he said, chewing his lip. "But you can kiss any hope of keeping our position disguised goodbye."

She ran her hands through her close-cropped hair. "I don't care."

Pollard fiddled with the controls, and a moment later the screen changed to a pixilated broadcast of an empty street. "I think this is Moscow," Pollard whispered.

Cyrillic lettering scrolled across the bottom of the screen. "Do you speak any Russian?" Hollister asked.

"Nyet," Pollard said, shaking his head. "I took a semester at the academy, but that was a long time ago."

"I was afraid of that…" She leaned forward. "Can you turn up the volume?"

Pollard double-checked. "It's all the way up."

"Try another channel."

As he reached for the switch, Hollister grabbed his forearm. "Wait!" Pollard withdrew his hand. "What's that?" She pointed at the side of the screen where a figure had entered the frame.

They leaned in closer to get a better view. The figure resolved itself to a man after a moment. He was staggering directly toward the camera. There was no intelligence in his eyes, no awareness he was being watched.

"Something's wrong with him," Pollard murmured.

Hollister squinted. "I think you're right..."

As the man drew closer, Hollister gasped. The man, or what was left of him, was a patchwork of flesh and bone, a gnawed travesty of something that should by all accounts be dead. A gaping hole in his midsection glistened in the murky twilight, a slick, hollow cavity devoid of life-sustaining organs. Yet he was walking, moving about as if out for a pleasant stroll.

Hollister and Pollard watched in silence as the man reached the camera and then passed it, going out of view. In the distance, more figures appeared. A healthy-looking young woman sprinted into the frame from somewhere behind the camera. She stopped in the middle of the street and looked around as if searching for a place to hide. Then, she darted from one locked door to another. She turned her head as if she had heard something, and then raced off in the opposite direction.

A moment later, a group of fifty or sixty of the walking wounded entered the camera's view, moving in the same direction as the woman. They seemed to focus as one, moving in lockstep. A minute later, they disappeared around a corner and were gone.

Hollister cracked her knuckles. "Can you get CNN International?"

"Sure. Hold on a second." Pollard adjusted the frequency. The screen snapped to life, all traces of pixilation gone. The familiar CNN banner filled the screen. A line of blinking text underneath said 'Feed Unavailable.' That was enough for Hollister. Something had happened on the surface, something terrible.

She fixed Pollard with a stare. "Take us to launch depth. Proceed with launch on my authority, Commander Code 83889348HHY-44BN." Andrew gulped and began relaying her orders.

From her seat, Hollister felt the ship pitch forward, nosing back into the welcome embrace of the ocean.

Not yet an epitaph

I am homesick after mine own kind,
Oh I know that there are folk about me, friendly faces,
But I am homesick after mine own kind.

Ezra Pound, In Durance

Fourteen

Three Months Later

Megan stretched and stifled a yawn. She scrubbed a stray bead of sweat from her forehead and wiped it on her pillow. Through the window, she could see the sun starting to sink behind the Tucson Mountains, far across the valley. The last rays of the day flooded her room with a toasty orange glow that reminded her of a dying campfire. Despite the hour, it was still hot. The heat was a dense blanket of misery crushing her spirit, draining every last bit of motivation from her soul. The best she could hope for was to lie still and wait for the relative coolness of evening. Even then, true relief would only arrive in the final hours before dawn, after the heat of the previous day had finally radiated into the night sky.

Whoever invented the concept of hell must have lived in the desert, she mused. To make matters worse, there was the dust. No matter what she did, no matter how much she washed, she couldn't rid herself of the feeling she was covered with a fine layer of the stuff. It got into everything, her bed, the food, even the water.

She sighed and rolled onto her stomach. At least I'm not alone… She chuckled.

For reasons she hadn't yet been able to determine, the undead seemed to suffer from the heat as much, if not more, than the living. Not all of them, of course. There were always pockets of the bastards, the outliers, who didn't obey the rules. They were the ones to watch out for. They would sneak up on you during a supply run and take a chunk out of your ass, putting an end to your miserable existence in a hurry.

There was a knock at her door, a gentle, back-of–the-knuckles rapping. She tensed instinctively, forgetting for a moment where she was, thinking she was back in the brothel and a client was outside her door waiting for his session. She breathed out and forced herself to relax. Came back to the present. Those days are over. Never again. She rolled over and ran her fingers through her hair, smoothing it back. "Come in!"

The door creaked open a few inches, and a smiling brown face peered through the gap. "Megan?"

She sat up. "Everyone's here," Cesar Aguilar announced. "Are you ready?"

Something in his tone, the tentative nature of his question, took her back to the first time they had met. Megan's car had died as the bombs fell on Las Vegas, the engine falling silent as the electromagnetic pulse scrambled the complex electronics embedded within. It was only blind luck that she had been stretched across the seat searching for the instruction manual in the glove box when the sky caught fire. Five seconds earlier and she would have lost her sight to the blast.

With nowhere else to go, she had set out on foot, heading south to her sister Chloe's place in Arizona. The trip was uneventful except for one night south of Flagstaff when she had encountered a group of three men heading in the opposite direction. Megan was sleeping in an abandoned minivan on the side of the highway when she was suddenly awakened by a beam of light stabbing into her eyes. A man's face leered at her through the window. A live man.

Fearing the worst, she had grabbed a tire iron and scrambled out the other side of the vehicle, only to land in the arms of a burly man with an iron grip. He snatched her weapon and tossed it to another man she couldn't see, and then he had spun her around and slammed her against the side of the van. He grabbed her wrists, squeezing them together so hard she thought they would break.

"Are you bitten?" he demanded, his voice dripping with malice and a hint of fear.

Megan shook her head. "No."

"Check her," another man said, a little too enthusiastically. Visions of rape and murder raced through her mind, paralyzing her. A few minutes later, it was all over. The man with the iron grip stepped away and turned his back as she began to dress.

"We had to be sure," he said apologetically. Megan fumed with anger, yet she understood. A bite was a death sentence.

The men had turned out to be part of a small community of survivalists holed up a few miles down the road. Megan was the first live person they had seen in weeks, and they were desperate for news from the outside world.

The next morning, Megan had set off with a pistol, a backpack full of food, two plastic milk jugs full of water, and assurances from the community that she was welcome to return if she didn't find what she was looking for. It wasn't until she had reached the outskirts of Tucson that she realized the error of her decision. The city was crawling with undead. They were everywhere she looked. The elements had taken their toll on many, reducing them to desiccated fragments of their former selves. Yet, they were still as hungry as ever, dragging themselves through the sand-swept streets in search of their next meal.

Chloe lived in the northern foothills. *Had lived.* But by the time Megan arrived, the only thing left of her sister's house was blackened hillside and a charred foundation; an out-of-control brushfire had taken everything. Chloe and her family were nowhere to be found.

By that point, she was exhausted, and she had nowhere else to go. She had to make a choice. While the undead owned the core of the city, their numbers were sparse along the outskirts. Megan figured as long as she was careful, she could exist on the margins for a while, could continue to survive on scavenged supplies until she figured out her next steps.

She set her sights on Scorpion Canyon, located on the far northeast side. According to the *Welcome to Tucson* guidebook she had liberated from an abandoned gas station, it had water year-round and was riddled with trails she could use in the event of a zombie attack.

When she arrived at the low-slung ranger station on the edge of the canyon, she wasn't surprised to find it locked and abandoned. A few minutes later, with the assistance of a large rock from the parking lot, she was inside, gorging herself on half-melted granola bars and bottled water.

She had settled into her new home quickly. Being on her own, she needed little in the way of food. The worst part was the heat and the boredom. She solved the boredom with a cache of paperbacks liberated from a truck in the parking lot. The heat she would have to live with. Air conditioning was a distant memory.

Cesar had come into her life during her first foray from the ranger station. It was early morning, and she was nearing an abandoned convenience store when three people burst from the desert and dashed across the road directly in front of her. As she watched in mute shock, they plunged into the brush on the opposite side and kept going without even acknowledging her. Megan had come to an abrupt stop, unable to believe what she had just seen. Then she set off in pursuit. "Hey!" she yelled. "Wait up!" By the time she caught up, she was panting like a dog and her thighs were chafed raw from her shorts.

The people were filthy, layered in grime from head to toe. Tattered clothes and frayed backpacks told the story of a life on the run. Most telling of all were their faces. Every one of them shared a look of sheer terror, a manic fight-or-flight stare that set her nerves jangling.

She bent over, hands on her knees, and tried to catch her breath. "Who..." she gulped, trying to recover, "are you?"

A short Hispanic man had gestured past her shoulder, in the direction from which they had just come. "We have to move. There are many undead behind us."

It took a second for Megan to digest what he was saying. "How many?" she finally asked.

He shifted his gaze between her and his traveling companions. "Too many." They ran.

That day now felt like ancient history. Since then, their numbers had grown by leaps and bounds as word spread amongst the survivors remaining in the city. A hundred and three people now called the Scorpion canyon ranger station home. Most importantly, they were no longer running.

"Megan?"

"Yeah. I'm coming." She collected her notebook from beside the bed and climbed to her feet. She followed Cesar down the hall, making her way to the front of the house. Unscented candles flickered in the main room, casting dancing shadows on the walls.

"Hey, guys," Megan said sheepishly.

Seated in front of her on a collection of plush leather couches were most of the other members of the Scorpion Canyon Leadership Council. Fellow survivors and refugees, they were her most trusted friends and confidantes, people with whom she routinely entrusted not only her life, but the lives of the myriad other people living in the compound.

"She rises!" exclaimed a shaggy-haired man of about fifty.

Megan gave him an annoyed grin. "Very funny, Pringle."

Mike Pringle, or 'Pringle' as he liked to be called, threw back his head and guffawed. "I'm just busting your balls, Megan." Megan bit her tongue, resisting the urge to snap at him. Pringle was always busting someone's balls.

Six weeks earlier, she and Cesar had found Pringle on the side of I-10, just north of town. Her first impression had been that he was hanging on by a thread, that he was a drifter who would move on in a few days. She was wrong. Within a week, Pringle began to relax, to become part of the community. He was staying. Megan still didn't know his whole story, only that he had been an airline pilot before, and that he had been flying the day the dead rose. Every time she pressed him on how he had survived, he changed the subject. What she did know was that he had a good head on his shoulders despite his acidic tongue and his initial clumsy attempts to get into her pants. She trusted him. For the most part.

Cesar positioned himself on the arm of an easy chair, an almost imperceptible groan escaping as he eased himself down. *His back.* Megan's fingers found a three-inch scar on her left arm and rubbed it. Like everyone else, she had her own battle marks from the war for survival.

She took Cesar's cue, found a spot on an opposing couch, and tucked her feet beneath her. The air in the room felt charged, as if everyone was holding their breath, waiting.

Cesar coughed into his hand. "I'd like to start by thanking you all for coming over tonight," he began. "I know we have a lot to do for tomorrow, but this is important."

Megan knew what was coming. Cesar had briefed her on his plans, using her as a sounding board. "I'm going to cut straight to the point," he continued.

Pringle shifted in his seat, straightened up and leaned forward. "Well, let's get on with it, amigo."

A slight frown, gone before it could gain purchase, flitted across Cesar's lips. Megan knew he hated it when Pringle called him that, knew how much he bristled at being stereotyped because of the color of his skin.

"We're staying the course," Cesar announced. No build-up. No preamble.

Pringle reclined and flicked a non-existent piece of dirt from his knee. "I don't think that's such a good idea Cesar."

Megan's face grew warm. She shared a sidelong glance with Cesar. "What do you mean?"

Pringle let out an exasperated sigh. "We've gone over this a million times." He stood and walked to the window. "We've grown too fast. We've got too many people for the supplies on hand. We can't keep this up." He turned back to face them.

Megan opened her mouth, but Pringle cut her off. "Plus, there's been an increase in undead traffic over the past few weeks. Hell, just yesterday we found two of them just down the road, heading toward the gate."

"And we stopped them," Cesar interjected, "As we always do."

Pringle pointed at him. "If you had balls, Cesar, you would have said no to all of these additional people. We were fine at twenty, maybe even thirty. But now we've got a crisis on our hands. We've got people here who can't fight their way out of a paper bag, and we're somehow responsible for them. I'm sick and tired of it!" He took a menacing step toward Cesar.

"So that's what this is all about?" Cesar replied. "You want to turn people away? Tell them to fend for themselves?" Cesar's temper flared. "We will not turn anyone away!" Cesar said in slow, even words. "Not as long as I have any say in the matter."

Pringle's left eye twitched. Megan thought he was about to explode.

"That's what we're here for, isn't it Cesar? So we all have a say in the matter?" He puffed his chest out, towering over Cesar.

Megan leaped to her feet. "Guys! Back off," she demanded. "This is crazy!" She wedged herself between the men, and faced Pringle. "I hear what you're saying, Mike. You feel like we've taken on too many people, that we can't protect or defend them anymore." Pringle nodded slowly, his eyes full of suspicion.

She turned to Cesar. "And you believe we have a responsibility to protect anyone who wants to join us." She straightened to her full five-and-a-half feet. "I think I have an idea."

Cesar raised an eyebrow, and Mike looked skeptical.

She started to lay out her plan.

Fifteen

Hollister traced a chewed-to-the-quick nail up the thigh of the boy on her bed, winding her way through his wispy black pubic hair and finally stopping at the base of his cock. She wrapped a calloused palm around the shaft and began stroking it with singleminded intensity, increasing her pace as she felt him stiffen. The boy moaned and closed his eyes.

"Again?" he mouthed.

A salacious leer spread across her face. "Mmmm hmmm."

He opened his eyes and watched her work, his face a pathetic mask of revulsion and fatigue. Hollister knew he was worn out, expended. This was her third time in the past hour, after all. Not that she gave a shit. She slicked him down with her mouth, and then climbed on top, plunging herself against him in one brutal motion, burying him deep inside of her.

From her perch, she watched his face with rapt amusement. Faster and faster she moved, skin smacking against skin. Sweat dripped from her brow, splashing on his chest. The boy's eyes were closed, his mouth a tight grimace as she ground her pelvis against his, filling herself, taking what she had been denied for so long. She felt him going soft, slipping out of her—a sudden absence. He wouldn't meet her eyes.

With a disgusted groan, Hollister rolled off and flopped onto her back beside him. She pointed at the door. "Get out!" It wasn't an invitation.

The boy didn't wait for a second command. Cradling his abused penis, he rolled from the bed and gathered his clothes, then scurried from the room like a whipped dog.

Hollister lazed on the soiled sheets for a minute, reflecting on her evening. One thing was for sure. It was time for a new plaything. She chuckled to herself, amused at the beautiful absurdity of her life.

Prior to the collapse, this type of behavior would have landed her in the brig, or worse, in Leavenworth. Trapped on a ship full of young, virile men, she had often fantasized about starting at the bow and working her way to the stern, fucking her way through the crew one sailor at a time. But not as a Commander in the United States Navy. In a contest between her carnal desires and her passion for Navy life, the Navy had always come out on top. Besides, even if she had found a way to fulfill her fantasies in the civilian world, there would have been complications. There always were.

She recalled the instant she had given the order to fire. Not since the day she received her Navy commission at the Academy had she been so filled with possibility. It was the closest she had ever come to orgasm without a man inside of her, and it had taken everything in her power to maintain a somber face in front of Pollard. Her first priority was survival. The world was turning to shit, and she alone had the knowledge and the skills to survive. Sure, there would be others out there, people who could scavenge, read the winds, or build a campfire. *But did they have the desire to remake reality in their image?* She didn't think so.

She sat up and crossed her legs. The room reeked of sex and stale cigarettes, a musky, flat odor that both turned her on and made her nauseous. Still, it smelled better than the inside of a sub.

Her thoughts finally settling, she slid from the bed and pulled on a t-shirt, a pair of loose shorts, and a pair of battered New Balances. She was almost ready. Dipping her finger into a gallon-sized Ziploc on the nightstand, Hollister scooped out an ample pinch of cocaine. She put her finger to her left nostril and snorted, drawing the fine white powder deep into the recesses of her sinus cavity. Her heart responded immediately, hammering in her chest like a caged animal. The room jumped into a sharper focus; energy welled from deep within.

Fortified, she headed for the door. Her heart skipped a beat as she almost collided with Andrew Pollard, who had been waiting on the other side. *Had he been listening the entire time?*

She scowled. Pollard shot her a half-salute on top of a knowing leer. "I've got some news from the scouting party," he said.

She pushed past, jostling his arm in the process. Papers fluttered to the floor, and he bent to retrieve them.

"How long have you been here, Andrew?" she said, stopping and turning to face him.

"Not long." *He's lying.*

She paused for a moment, thinking back to the young man who had just left. "Please dispose of…" She couldn't remember his name. "The one who was just here. I'm finished with him."

"Consider it done."

She had a new toy in mind. "And make arrangements to bring me someone new tomorrow, maybe the Asian kid that came in with that group from Colorado last week."

"Of course," Pollard said. If Pollard had any reservations about serving as her pimp, he didn't let on. To the contrary, he seemed almost too eager.

"Okay. Let's hear about the scouting run," she said, taking off down the hall.

Pollard launched into a rundown of the mission. Fort Huachuca was a sprawling base nestled up against a mountain range, providing a natural barrier for the undead swarms migrating from south to north. Still, the post was a scene of devastation. Abandoned vehicles, flattened fences, and burned-out buildings dominated the landscape. Expended shell casings glinting like discarded diamonds lay scattered across the sun-baked desert floor, evidence of futile battles against an army that never retreated.

As with the military and police installations they had inspected as they traveled through Mexico, it appeared civilians had gravitated to the base in a last-ditch bid for protection. It had been the wrong choice. The soldiers were under orders to protect their base at all costs. Unfortunately for both parties, once the undead infection began spreading through a crowd, the chance of others in the crowd becoming infected grew exponentially. Everyone died. And then they came back.

Weapons and ammunition were readily available, Pollard reported, as was food.

The journey from decorated submarine captain to post-apocalypse survivor had not been without its challenges. When Hollister had grounded the Wyoming in Ensenada, she gave her crew the choice of either following her or going their own way. Most struck out on their own, embarking on personal suicide missions to find their families or die trying. Once the deserters were gone, Hollister had turned to her remaining crew and congratulated them on their decision. And then she laid down the new law of the land. She had executed all but seven of this original group within the first week, solidifying her role as alpha bitch of the new world. The remaining crew had fallen into line, afraid to question her, and now afraid to strike out on their own.

Hollister had the beginnings of a new army. She followed this strategy with everyone they encountered, offering protection and support in the form of food and weapons in exchange for absolute loyalty. Word of mouth served as a powerful motivator for new recruits. She had only executed two others since that day.

They reached the outside door of the warehouse, and she pushed through. Pollard followed, kicking a wedge of wood under the door to prop it open. Hollister fished a pack of cigarettes from her pocket and shook one out. She didn't offer one to Pollard. She was excited by the potential of a base full of weapons, but also a little overwhelmed. The extent of the destruction was far greater than she had expected, and she worried about the challenges that lay ahead.

She blew smoke in Pollard's face and smiled as he winced. "It's too fucking hot here," she spat. "We need to get out of the desert." Pollard looked as if he was about to speak, but said nothing.

She sensed his mood. "Yeah, I know. Southern Arizona, and all that. I've got no one to blame but myself…"

Pollard rewarded her with a thin smile. "We can be on the road in twenty-four hours," he offered.

"No." She knew he meant well. They had adequate fuel and supplies. They had scavenged vehicles in Mexico, vintage cars and trucks built before the proliferation of EMP-sensitive electronics.

Pollard raised his eyebrows. "No?"

"I want to send a scouting team into Tucson before we head out, to see if there's anything we can use." Tucson hadn't been on her sub's targeting menu, and there was no guarantee another boat, or even a land-based missile, hadn't been targeted at the city of a million. If, however, the city still existed, it would make their journey that much easier. They might even get lucky and find a military aircraft hardened against EMP. If it was gone, a barren crater, she would add one more 'X' to her map of dead zones.

Pollard nodded. "Okay. Tucson it is. I'll get things rolling."

Hollister finished her cigarette and flicked the butt toward a clump of prickly pear cactus where it became stuck on a spine, alongside dozens of others. She grinned, pleased with her aim.

Things are coming together.

Sixteen

Taos, New Mexico

Jack watched the candle in the center of the table flicker, the pool of wax around the wick glistening in the soft yellow light. He sighed and put his head in his hands. Across the room, Becka and Ellie were curled together, slumbering under a stained sleeping bag. He wore a dingy, blue t-shirt and jeans. His clothes were stiff with accumulated sweat and grime from the past few weeks. He didn't care. At least he smelled better than the undead. His thoughts drifted to the moment when he realized how truly screwed humanity was.

After a frantic race to his mother's house to retrieve the children, he and Becka had spent the next four hours huddled in front of the television, unable to tear themselves away from the macabre images of people attacking and consuming each other in the streets. It was only when the screen went blank and the emergency broadcast tone started blaring that they were able to focus on their situation.

The ski town of Taos, New Mexico was about as far from civilization as you could get and still have modern amenities, and that was its only saving grace. The message that had scrolled by on the bottom of the television screen instructing people to evacuate large cities and keep clear of the *changed,* even if they were family members, seemed surreal at the time, like something from a bad B-movie. *Changed.* That was what the media called the undead. *Stupid name*, Jack thought in hindsight. They were zombies, pure and simple. They were the very same creatures he and his friends in high school had laughed at as they consumed legions of hapless teenagers while stumbling around like brain-dead robots in all of those silly movies. He wasn't laughing anymore, and he was sure his friends, if they were still alive, weren't laughing either.

These creatures were the real deal, worse than anything George Romero could have ever dreamed up. And they didn't shamble. No, these sons of bitches could sprint when they wanted to, at least some of them. And sometimes they were even able to work doors and windows, just like when they had been alive. He felt a momentary twinge of pity for all of the people who had perished trying to reach safety by following the half-baked evacuation orders proposed by the government. Jack had always known in the back of his mind that the west was home to a large portion of the country's strategic missile forces. But for some reason, he had assumed they were all up north somewhere—Montana, Wyoming, Kansas, maybe even Colorado, but not in New Mexico.

But when the missiles lanced up on the horizon, bright plumes of fire defining their westward trajectories, the reality had smacked him in the face, forcing him to reevaluate everything he believed about the place he had called home. California, he thought. The big cities. Los Angeles. Sacramento. San Francisco. A few minutes later there were a series of chalky-white flashes to the far north, in Colorado—Denver, Colorado Springs, and Pueblo, most likely. And there was at least one large flash to the southeast, Albuquerque. But none for Taos. For that, Jack was thankful.

For everything else, he was furious—because the government's plan didn't work. The zombies still came. Only now, in addition to an insatiable hunger for human flesh, they were walking dirty bombs.

He wondered about the rest of the world. According to the news before the power had failed, the undead were on the march across the globe. Europe. China. Africa. The Middle East. Everywhere. He supposed there were others like his family scattered about. Between the nuclear-armed countries, there weren't enough missiles to destroy the entire world—or were there? He didn't know anymore. Since the collapse of the cold war, he had stopped paying attention to the whole concept of nuclear Armageddon. Big mistake.

The first zombie had arrived in Taos a week after the bombs fell. It came from somewhere near Albuquerque, maybe closer, and it was in remarkably good condition. In fact, Jack hadn't even realized it was a zombie until it was almost too late. The creature had strolled down the long driveway to his house with its head swiveling left and right, as if looking for someone. His gait appeared normal enough. The thing that tipped Jack off was the man's clothing, or lack thereof. He wore no shirt, a pair of cutoff jeans, and one flip-flop, as if he had wandered off from a backyard barbecue. How the flip-flop had stayed on the man's foot for so long still puzzled Jack.

Madeline had noticed him first. "Daddy. There's a man outside." Nothing in her voice indicated alarm. He and Becka had done their best to shield the twins from what was going on around them. They knew it couldn't last forever, that things had changed irrevocably, but they wanted to delay it as long as possible. That was another mistake, it turned out.

The man noticed them, and like a missile locking onto a target, he had changed direction, heading toward the back porch where they all sat.

Jack stood. "Can I help you?"

The man hadn't said anything; he just kept coming.

Then Jack saw it. There was a small hole in the man's chest, a few inches below his left nipple. A line of dried blood snaked down his stomach and around to his back at his waistline.

"Becka! Mom! Get the kids inside. Now!" he yelled. Becka hadn't wasted a second in herding the girls through the front door.

"Stop right there!" Jack commanded. The man was thirty feet out and accelerating—almost running. "I said stop!" Jack felt the world closing in around him. Time slowed to a crawl. He picked up his Benelli hunting rifle and brought it to his shoulder, leveled the barrel in the man's direction and curled his finger around the trigger. It had been Becka's idea to keep a gun close by at all times.

The feel of the cool, slightly oily steel under his index finger sent a wave of calm through Jack's shaking arms. "I can do this," he said under his breath.

"Stop right there!" he yelled. "This is your last warning!" He centered the man's head in his crosshairs. The man opened his mouth and let loose a moan, a low, almost subsonic, guttural roar that made the hairs on Jack's neck leap to attention.

He squeezed. The gun boomed, and the recoil punched him in the shoulder. The man had stopped in his tracks as the bullet tore through his cranium, turning his head into an airborne mist of bone and congealed blood, fanning out across the yard behind him. He stumbled forward a few more steps before tumbling into the dirt less than five feet from the edge of the porch. Jack lowered the gun and exhaled. So this is it. Behind him, the girls wailed in terror.

Jack had then descended the porch stairs, the boards he had laid so carefully the previous summer squeaking under each step. The man—no, the creature—wasn't moving. Brain and skull fragments spread out behind its body, coating the grass with a glistening slick of red, black, and gray. Chunks of skull poked up like spring mushrooms after a rainstorm. Jack slung his rifle over his shoulder and grabbed the garden hoe from the porch railing.

"Jack? Are you okay?" The door opened behind him, and Becka stepped out.

He motioned for her to get back inside. "Yeah. Stay inside, Becka."

He approached the body. Circling around the corpse, he realized the man was in worse shape than he initially thought. He almost gagged at the putrid stench rising from the body, and had pulled his shirt over his nose to block the scent.

The creature's hand twitched, and Jack took a quick step back. As he stared, the fingers opened and closed, grasping at the air. Fuck…He leaned the hoe against the porch and put the gun back to his shoulder. Taking another step back, he fired another round into what was left of the creature's head. He was ready for the kick that time. The body jerked once and then was still. There was nothing recognizable as a head above the neck then, only a bloody, dirty pulp.

He retrieved the hoe and poked the corpse one more time to make sure it was really dead.

What the hell do I do now? He didn't know if the blood was contagious, but he thought it might be. He hadn't really known anything. He sensed movement behind him and spun around.

Becka was at the foot of the stairs. His mother and the twins were at the door with their mouths agape. Jack dropped the hoe and went to Becka, folding her into his arms.

It hadn't taken long for more ghouls to arrive. It started with a trickle and grew to an outright flood in no time, hundreds of them in every condition imaginable, swarming through Taos in search of a new food source.

Jack had no way to check for radioactivity. Some were obviously carriers, burned and blackened, skin hanging in strips with bits of skeleton showing through. Those, he shot from a distance whenever possible. Then, miraculously, the wave had subsided. The undead passed them by. They had all breathed a mistaken sigh of relief and started trying to get their lives back to normal, whatever normal was after the end of the world.

Jack cursed himself to this day for letting his guard down. It was only two weeks after the last zombies passed that he had lost his mother and Maddie. He squeezed his eyes shut, trying to halt his recollection of that awful day.

It had started off gray and overcast, colder than usual for late summer, but not unheard of. The twins, as usual, were cute balls of fleece and mittens playing under the watchful eyes of their mother and grandmother. Jack was in the cellar, taking inventory of their food. There were plenty of canned vegetables from Becka's garden and ample dried food from their last run to Walmart. A generous neighbor had set them up with dried elk before the uprising, enough for the winter ahead. He was in the midst of calculating ration scenarios on a legal pad when he heard the first scream.

Dropping the notebook, he took the stairs two at a time, hoping and praying it wasn't what he thought it was. He was outside in a second, turning his head every which way, trying to find the source of the screams. Someone fired a small handgun, the *pop pop pop* sounds underscoring each scream. *Becka.*

Drawing the SIG Sauer P-229 from the paddle holster attached to the small of his back, he raced to the rear of the house. As he rounded the south corner, he saw the cause of the commotion.

Maddie was on the ground, clutching her forearm and crying. Jack's mother lay sprawled behind her, blood gushing from a tear in her throat. A few feet beyond, two zombies riddled with bullet holes lay on the ground. Becka was locked in a shooters stance with Ellie cowering behind her, one arm wrapped around her mother's leg and the other clasping her favorite blue teddy bear. She was whimpering, peering around Becka's leg at the dead ghouls.

Jack raced to Maddie. Her arm was bleeding, but she was otherwise uninjured. "I need to check on Grandma," he said. Maddie had nodded at him between sobs.

His mother was already gone. Jack's pulse, racing at a million miles an hour, had gone into overdrive. If it beat any faster, he feared it would burst from his chest and explode all over the room. *She's infected; she'll turn any second now.* He pushed the thought away and turned his attention back to his daughter. "Are you hurt, honey?" he asked. "Did they bite you?" *Please don't let her be bitten. Please. Please.* "Let me see your arm." She held it out reluctantly.

Jack's stomach dropped through the ground like a runaway elevator plunging into a pitch dark mineshaft. There was a perfect circular bite wound high on her right forearm. Bone glistened inside. Around the bite, the skin was an angry purple, bruised and crushed by human teeth. Becka came to his side, her pistol at the ready. She split her attention between Jack and Maddie and the surrounding yard, scanning for more zombies.

"It hurts, Daddy," Maddie cried through clenched teeth. "It hurts..." Jack didn't know how long it would take for her to turn. But he knew it was inevitable. Bites were one hundred percent fatal.

"Jack!" Becka said, a note of urgency in her voice. "Your mother." He glanced over his shoulder and saw his mother's hands and feet twitching. *That was fast.* Taking Maddie by her good arm, he guided her away, scooping Ellie up as he passed. As he walked by Becka, he mouthed the word "Please" and gestured at his mother's body.

Becka gave him an almost imperceptible nod of acknowledgement. As quickly as he could, Jack bundled the girls across the huge wraparound front porch and back inside the house. He had kicked the door closed with his heel just as Becka's gun *cracked.*

Jack felt a little piece of himself die with the sound. But at that moment, he didn't have time to mourn. He had to figure out what to do about his daughter. And the clock was ticking.

Becka had come inside a few minutes later, her face full of grim resolve. She placed her pistol on the dark mahogany table, the same table that was in Jack's grandmother's house when he was a child, and walked stiffly to the couch where Jack sat with the girls. Jack rubbed Maddie's back and murmured soothing words to calm her. It wasn't working. Ellie, meanwhile, stood a few feet away, unsure of what was going on.

"I'm sorry, Jack," Becka whsipered. Jack nodded and snorted back a tear. He would mourn his mother later.

Becka knelt in front of Maddie, gazed into her eyes. "I'm here now, honey."

Maddie pulled from Jack's arms and buried herself in her mother's breast. Becka squirmed, angling her body in an attempt to avoid contact with her daughter's infected blood.

"I'm so cold, Mommy," Maddie cried. "It hurts..."

"My baby. Oh, my baby." Becka sobbed into Maddie's hair before regaining her composure and stiffening up. Jack saw hardness in her eyes that scared him to his core.

"I don't know how long we have," he mouthed.

Becka nodded, still unable to speak.

"Is Maddie gonna to be okay?" Ellie squeaked. Becka looked at Jack with pleading eyes. She couldn't bring herself to answer her daughter. Not yet.

With a sudden jerk, Madeline grew stiff, as if stuck by lightning, and then she sagged in Becka's arms, limp as a rag doll. Becka lowered her to the floor. "It's happening." Tears brimming in her eyes, her mouth set in a grim line, she looked up at Jack.

Jack jumped to his feet, his mind struggling to comprehend how they had gotten to this place. He had no idea what to do, or even if there was anything he could do. He scanned the room, searching for some way to restrain Maddie, some way to avoid putting a bullet in her head like a diseased animal. *Like Mom.*

Maybe the infection will run its course...Maybe it won't affect her the way it does everyone else... He knew he was avoiding the inevitable. A simple bite wouldn't cause a person to go stiff, to pass out. Maddie was infected, and she was going to turn soon.

Jack pointed at the rear of the house. "Ellie! Go to your room and lock the door! Don't come out until I call you!" Ellie looked uncertain, began crying harder.

"I don't want to, Daddy. I want Maddie to be okay." She was shaking like the last leaf on a tree, threatening to blow away forever.

"Ellie! Do as your father says!" Becka commanded in her sternest mother voice. "Right now, young lady!" Ellie's tears increased, her whole body convulsing with sobs as she tore her gaze between her sister and her parents. With a glare of condemnation that broke Jack's heart, she turned and fled to her room, slamming the door shut behind her.

Jack stared at Maddie, knowing full well she was about to become a zombie. Her skin was already losing its ruddy tone, changing to a sallow gray as her body shut down.

"She's gone, Jack."

He looked up, surprised at the finality in Becka's voice. He wiped his eyes with the back of his hand. "I know... but I can't do it."

"Jack."

In his mind's eye, he saw the days and hours from Maddie's birth up until this awful moment. He tasted salt on the back of his throat, his eyes burned, he felt like he was about to vomit.

Becka put a hand on his shoulder.

Their eyes met. Only for a moment, but it was enough.

"Okay. Get her feet," he said.

Together they had carried their daughter from the house to the rear of the wood shed. Jack had chosen, the shed because there was no way Ellie could see it from inside the house. As gently as he could, he placed Maddie on the ground, propping her against a log he had been meaning to split all summer. She was so small and delicate she didn't even reach the top. She started to slump to the side, but Becka caught her, straightening her and making sure she was planted firmly against the tree. She kissed the top of Maddie's head and sat back on her haunches with her eyes closed.

Maddie jerked, her leg skittering a few inches to the side. "Becka!" Jack cautioned. "Watch out!"

Becka stood quickly and moved to his side. She clutched his arm. Jack withdrew his pistol. The metal was cold in his hands. A blocky chunk of death and destruction being put to a use he had never imagined in his worst nightmares. They embraced quickly, squeezing each other with all of their might. Jack never wanted to let go.

Maddie stirred again, and Jack broke their embrace. He took a step back and sighted on the thing that used to be his daughter. Becka sniffed and turned away. His grip on the pistol was sweaty and the gun wavered. He forced himself to focus.

Maddie's eyes twitched under their lids as the disease worked to figured out how to operate its new host.

Then they opened.

Jack's gun went off with a deafening roar, scattering the remains of his previous life to the winds and ushering in the brutal reality of the new.

Seventeen

The sun was finally below the mountains. Candles flickered softly, creating a sense of intimacy in the room—a warm bubble perfect for the discussion at hand.

"You're both right," Megan said.

Pringle frowned. "What makes you say that?" Cesar remained silent, a smile tugging at the corners of his mouth. The door creaked opened and Alicia entered.

"Hey, Alicia," Megan said.

"Sorry I'm late." Alicia took a seat on the far end of the couch.

Megan pressed on. "Where was I? Oh, yeah. I agree we've grown too fast. I mean, look at us. We've got all of these people jammed in here, and only a few who know what the hell they're doing."

"That's an understatement," Pringle spat out, squaring his shoulders for battle. Megan gave him a nod of encouragement. Engaging him was the key. He needed to debate. It was in his nature.

"Yes. It is, and I'm sorry for oversimplifying things. The four of us have been carrying this community on our backs since the start. As much as we want it to succeed, we're doomed if we don't change." Pringle nodded in enthusiastic agreement.

"But..." Megan's voice dropped an octave, becoming deadly serious. "We can't turn people away, not without giving them a choice. That's not who we are. It's not who I want us to become." She paused, letting her words hang in the air for emphasis. "We've got a good thing here. We've got a steady food supply, a decent climate, excluding the summers, and access to a city that wasn't leveled by nukes..." In an uncharacteristic move, Pringle didn't object, instead sinking into his seat and giving her his full attention.

"When was the last time a swarm passed this way?" Megan asked.

"Never," Pringle admitted.

"That's right. Never. The undead aren't bothering us. The only time we ever see them on this side of town is when they stray from their pack."

Cesar shifted in his chair and coughed into his hand. "We will have rules," he said, taking over from Megan. "Strong rules. Everyone will have responsibilities that they must fulfill if they wish to remain. I know many of the refugees are reluctant to venture into the dead zones, but that can't continue. We have to spread the risk..."

"And limit the number of newcomers?" Pringle asked, warming up to the idea.

Cesar shook his head. "No. We don't impose limits. Not yet, at least. However, we will require that anyone who joins us agrees to our rules. If they don't, then we'll send them on their way without exception."

Pringle chewed on this for a moment before responding. "How do you enforce these new rules?"

"That's where you come in. I want you to be in charge of implementing them, ensuring that they're fair for everyone in the compound." *Here's the carrot*, Megan thought.

Pringle's face lit up. Up until now, his responsibilities had been largely undefined. From collecting supplies to shooting undead stragglers and checking for infection in the inbound population, he did it all.

Cesar continued, "The key, Mike, is fairness. These rules don't mean a thing if they're not applied to everyone. And as much as I hate it, we'll have to turn people away at some point. We'll probably have to eject a few as well when they don't hold up their end of the bargain."

"I can think of a handful that we should send packing right now," Pringle said bitterly.

"He's right," Alicia said, breaking her silence. "Just yesterday I got into it with a guy who left the gate unguarded while he took a leak."

Megan turned to her. "You're kidding."

"I wish I was." Alicia sat up straighter. "And that wasn't the first time. We can't afford that type of attitude. If someone screws up like that, my opinion is they're out of here. No exceptions."

Cesar held up his hand. "I understand your frustration, Alicia. We'll take care of it."

Pringle's face took on a pained expression. It was clear he had some bones to pick—that he was hoping he could get rid of some particularly useless people. "Okay," he agreed finally. "I'll give the newcomers a chance to shape up. One chance."

Cesar stood and put out his hand. Pringle took it, and they shook, their disagreement buried for the moment. Megan breathed a silent sigh of relief. She knew that the last part pained Cesar. The thought of banishing anyone was anathema to him. Cesar believed every man, woman, and child could contribute to the community if given a chance, and the notion that someone would choose the alternative just didn't factor into his worldview. After all, it took only one person not taking their guard duties seriously to allow one of the undead inside the perimeter. Once that happened, things would move too fast for anyone to react. They could all be dead or infected within a matter of minutes.

"I think I can make this work," Pringle added. "I mean, it's a good step toward what I was thinking." He scratched his chin. "What about...? Never mind."

Cesar raised an eyebrow. "What is it, Mike?"

Pringle shook his head and stared off into the distance. "It's nothing."

Cesar narrowed his eyes. "Okay then. I'm glad we were able to come to a resolution. This," he gestured toward the window, "is too important for us to fight among ourselves. It's all we have left."

Megan stood. "Is anyone ready for a beer?" It was time to celebrate before the hard work began.

Eighteen

Kevin Salerno ran a torn piece of t-shirt along the barrel of his pistol, taking care to catch all the oil he could see in the glow from his red LED flashlight. His other pistol, a .22, lay on the table beside his right knee, ready in case he needed it. The boy scouts had been right all along. *Always be prepared.* In four practiced motions, he reassembled the pistol, jammed in a fresh fourteen-round magazine, and chambered a round. He clicked the safety on. Done.

He set the pistol aside, picked up the .22, and began taking it apart by memory. He took a deep breath, rolled his shoulders, and listened for his pulse. The process of cleaning his guns always stirred up conflicting emotions. On one hand, he felt an overwhelming sense of calm, a meditative peace in which everything else in his life faded into the background. Disassemble the weapon, clean it, apply oil, wipe, and then reassemble. Simple, repeatable, and predictable. At the same time, by the time he was finished, he always had a raging hard-on and wanted to fuck. This reaction had embarrassed him until his shrink told him it was normal, something to do with power.

He rolled his shoulders again, cracked his neck, then listened for sounds from outside. *No change.* A few minutes later, he was done with the second weapon. It went into the holster strapped on his thigh. He picked up the first pistol and went to the window. He peered outside. Although it was dark, he sensed movement around him, a lurking presence, rustling, shifting, ebbing and flowing like a deep, raging river. It was a swarm of the undead, the biggest he had ever seen.

Kevin was camped on the top floor of a mostly-complete condominium complex in Marana, just north of Tucson. Loading his motorcycle with camping gear and bugging out of town before things completely fell apart, he had barely escaped from Boise as the zombie uprising mushroomed out of control. It didn't take a rocket scientist to realize the extent of what was happening to the world, and he correctly figured the best place to be was anywhere but a major city. He had watched the bombs fall from the side of I-25, weeping uncontrollably as they blanketed his beloved western landscape with brilliant, incandescent flashes and far-off rumbles. The only direction untouched by the bombs was south, so that was where he had headed.

Now that he was there, at the far corner of what remained of the United States, he was second-guessing his decision. There were a lot of undead, far more than he ever expected. It hadn't been that way when he arrived. When he first rolled into town, he was pleasantly surprised to discover only a few stragglers. He avoided them easily, collecting supplies for the next leg of his trip and allowing himself to relax for the first time in as long as he could remember.

Tucson seemed as good a place as any to take a break, to figure out what to do next—keep going south into Mexico, or head east into New Mexico, Texas, and the Gulf Coast beyond.

But then the undead had arrived. Where they were from, he didn't know, and it didn't matter at that point. What did matter was that the swarm seemed to have no end. Thousands upon thousands of undead milled just outside his door. He imagined what it would look like from the air, probably like the great wildebeest migrations in Africa.

He wasn't able to discern any sort of pattern from his hideout; he couldn't tell if the swarm would eventually pass by or if it was circling back on itself, a hurricane of rotting flesh. Maybe there wasn't a pattern; maybe they communicated telepathically, or through their moans. He had no fucking idea.

He crept back from the window and returned to the enormous master bathroom where he had set up camp. Big enough for a couch and his pack, the bathroom served as an adequate hideout in the midst of what was most definitely hostile territory.

The noise was the worst part, a constant rustling, the occasional crash as one of the creatures bumped into something. Fortunately, they didn't moan unless they saw something they wanted to eat, and thank God, that hadn't happened. Yet. It freaked him out, put him on edge, and messed with his head. At any moment, one of them could catch his scent, and he would be screwed, with nowhere left to run. He shuddered at the thought. He had long ago decided he would take his own life before he became dinner for one of those sick bastards.

Sinking into the couch, he put his feet up on the dressing table and scratched his forehead with the barrel of the loaded pistol. Before he knew what he was doing, the barrel had traced a line under his jaw and was pressing into the soft flesh of his throat. He caressed the trigger, running his finger along the delicate steel as he would touch a woman. *Why not?* he asked himself. *Why the fuck not?* He cocked the hammer. Dug in a little deeper. He scratched at the scruff on his jaw, bending the hairs backward and letting them snap back to attention one by one. It hurt, but in a good way. It reminded him he was still alive.

What else do I have to live for? He had no family to speak of. No wife. No girlfriend. No close friends, at least none that he knew were alive. His parents were both dead, and his brother had died in high school. He was alone in the world. *The last man standing.* He laughed, a thin, reedy cackle that to his ears sounded like someone else.

The trigger beckoned. Kevin exhaled and removed his finger. *Not today. Not now.* He eased the hammer down and lowered the gun, laying it on the couch cushion beside his leg. This had become a nightly ritual for him, and he was sure some day he would get the balls to pull the trigger. *But not today.*

Feeling around in the space under his feet, he retrieved his sleeping bag. He pulled it up and over himself, making sure to tuck it around his feet. He didn't like sleeping with his feet exposed. These days the monsters under the bed really would bite.

He was snoring within a minute.

~~~

Kevin awoke thrashing and bathed in sweat. Sun streamed between the partially open blinds, hot white lines slicing the room into equidistant pieces. *Fuck, it's hot.* Yawning, he staggered to his feet and shuffled to the window. He pulled the blinds back a fraction of an inch.

He blinked, unable to believe the sight before him. There wasn't a single undead in sight. The only evidence of their passing was a few twitching appendages and splattered stains, bodily fluids ground into the asphalt by tens of thousands of feet. He dashed over to the window on the far side of the condominium and peeked out. *Nothing. Where the hell did they all go?*
~~~

His internal clock told him it was around eight or nine. *When did they leave?* As hard as he tried, Kevin couldn't recall the moment he had finally fallen asleep. One minute he was curled up on the couch thinking about… something, and the next thing he knew, it was morning. He didn't like losing control like that, and he especially hated blacking out.

The passing of the horde brought both opportunity and a renewed sense of urgency. He was out of food, and he needed to get back on the road before they returned.

A few minutes later, carrying his backpack and his helmet in his left hand and his pistol in his right, he bounded down the stairs of the condo to the first floor. He put his eye up to the peephole and methodically checked the street in front of the house. The upper floors overhung the ground-level entry, creating a narrow carport barely big enough for a family sedan. *All clear.*

With as much stealth as he could muster, he unlatched the deadbolt and nudged the door open a crack. The leaves of a young fan palm rustled in the hot breeze, their woody shh shh the only thing he could hear. He listened for a moment and inhaled deeply, searching for the scent of rot. Still clear.

Nudging the door all the way open, he stepped outside, careful not to make any noise. The wind shifted, and with it came a sickly-sweet whiff of putrescent flesh, like a piece of forgotten beef jerky rotting on the floor of his car in the summer. Kevin flattened himself against the wall and raised his .45. *Why can't this ever be easy?*

The creature was trapped in the carport of the next condo unit, stuck between an oversized recycling bin and the front bumper of a faded-blue minivan. It was silent, staring in the other direction. *Waiting.*

Kevin crept to the edge of his carport and peered around the edge. The wind was in his favor for once. The street was clear in both directions. There were no others… that he could see. Hard experience told him where there was one, there would be more. Like deer, the undead traveled in threes.

Slipping his .45 into his leg holster, Kevin withdrew the.22 and clicked off the safety. It was a much quieter gun, perfect for up-close work and unlikely to draw other undead. Running on the balls of his feet, keeping his body low and out of sight, he dashed to the rear of the minivan. The zombie hadn't caught his scent yet.

He stuck his head around the side of the van and inspected the creature. One thing was clear; it was once a woman. Beyond that, he couldn't tell. Dark brown and leathery, wrinkled like an old shrunken head, this one was a wreck. Probably radioactive, he decided, noting random bald spots where the creature's hair had fallen out. He looked closer. *Ahh. That's why it can't move.* It was tangled in a garden hose coiled by the front wheel.

Kevin glanced over his shoulder, ensuring he had an escape route if things went bad. He tapped the muzzle of his pistol against the minivan. Once. Twice. The monster whipped its head around, teeth bared, nostrils flaring as it tried to capture his scent. Its arms came up, reaching for him. *Man, that's an ugly fucker*, Kevin thought as he aimed. *Must be from Phoenix.*

The creature opened its mouth to moan, but before it could make a sound, Kevin pulled the trigger twice. The bullets entered the creature's head through its left eye socket. They didn't come out the other side, instead rattling around like rocks in a can, liquefying the remains of its diseased brain like ice cream in a blender. The creature crumpled to the ground, finally at rest.

"Lights out," Kevin whispered. He checked his rear again. Still clear. A few minutes later, he was roaring south on his motorcycle.

Next stop, Tucson.

Nineteen

Cesar called the community together the next morning to announce the new rules. Everyone except those on fence patrol was required to attend. No exceptions.

Most took the news well. A few were upset, grumbling amongst themselves. Others seemed ambivalent, resigned to doing whatever was necessary to stay alive. It was about the mix of reactions Megan had expected.

Three brothers interrupted the speech halfway through, announcing they were moving on. They invited anyone who wanted to come to join them. They had no takers.

"We're better off on our own," the oldest brother insisted, the fear in his eyes betraying his bravado.

"Idiot," Pringle muttered under his breath. Megan jabbed an elbow into his ribs and hissed at him to keep it to himself, earning an angry glare in return.

The brothers, the last vestiges of a large fundamentalist Mormon enclave from western Arizona, were intent upon forming their own community. Megan couldn't fault them. The Scorpion Canyon community was composed of a ragtag mix of beliefs and backgrounds, and although Cesar was a devout Catholic, he took great pains to keep his religion out of daily life inside the fence. "It's not that I don't believe this is all part of God's plan," he had confessed to Megan one afternoon, "I just think he's taking a break now, dealing with something else more important."

His attitude had surprised Megan. It seemed somehow Buddhist, not at all what she expected. The statement had stuck with her, impressed her. It made her think about the future and what was in store for all of them, and for the people outside, survivors still living day-to-day on the margins of the ruined world. Megan had long ago abandoned the idea of a benevolent God. The zombie uprising had only served to solidify her conviction that humanity was on its own.

The first order of business after the announcement was a scavenging mission into town. They were running low on everything from food to ammunition. To Megan's great satisfaction, Cesar had to turn people away when he asked for volunteers. People were frightened of the undead, but they were more scared of being turned out.

Pringle had been unusually quiet throughout the whole meeting, continuously scanning the audience and observing body language, making notes on people who seemed eager to help and those who kept quiet. The meeting ran for another fifteen minutes, and when it finally broke up, the participants scattered, imbued with a new sense of purpose.

"About tomorrow..." Pringle said as they left the ranger station. She kept walking, motioning for him to follow. He sped up to match her pace. "I want to find a two-way radio while we're in town. A shortwave or something…"

Megan stopped and faced him. "That's a great idea, Mike. I bet there's one down there."

He met her eyes and stuck his hands in his pockets. "There have to be other people out there. I think it's time we start looking for them. Learn what's going on in the rest of the world..."

Megan nodded enthusiastically. "I think so, too. I'm sure Cesar will agree."

Pringle took his hands out and frowned. "I'm not asking for Cesar's permission, Megan."

That caught her off guard. "Oh. I'm sorry. That's not what I meant. Not at all."

"Are you sure?" Pringle asked. "Because if you are, then I may have been a little hasty in supporting him."

Megan touched his forearm. "I think it's a wonderful idea, Mike. Run with it. See what you can find."

Pringle moved his arm away from her touch. "I intend to."

Feeling like there was something else she should say, but unsure of how to vocalize it without sounding patronizing, Megan smiled and took off at a brisk pace for her quarters, leaving Pringle alone in the parking lot. She had a lot to do to get ready for the next day, and she was tired of dealing with his bullshit.

Twenty

The metal security door clanged shut behind Pollard as he stepped out of his trailer into the heat of midmorning. With a quick tug, he checked it to make sure it was securely latched. After sweeping most of the undead from the immediate vicinity, the last thing he wanted was for a straggler to wander into his house and surprise him. It still happened—had happened, in fact, only a week earlier.

Shielding his eyes, he set off at a brisk pace, heading southwest down the palm tree-lined street. The residential section quickly gave way to a commercial district, complete with the requisite cluster of big-box stores and row upon row of abandoned cars. Evidence of the undead rampage was everywhere. A ribcage, half-buried in a sand drift. Dark smears of gore baked into the pavement where people had been dragged from their vehicles and torn to shreds. Cars, filled with former undead, now sporting neat holes in their heads courtesy of his men.

His destination was the Home Depot the next block over. A hot wind pressed at his back. A tumbleweed rolled past, tiny branches *scritch scritching* the asphalt as it bounced over the curb and became momentarily stuck on a chain link fence. Pollard loved tumbleweeds.

He nodded at the two heavily armed men standing in front of the garden section as he approached. They straightened up and gave him their full attention. The older one saluted. The younger one stuffed a small black book with gold lettering on the cover—a bible, Pollard thought—into his back pocket.

Pollard waved him off. "At ease."

"Morning, Mr. Pollard," the younger man, really only a teen, said. The other man was much older, a former Army Ranger named Steve. Pollard didn't know either of them well.

"How's he doing?" he asked, looking past the men into the high fence of the garden section.

"Haven't heard a peep out of him all morning," the teen answered.

"Hmm. Let's take a look." He rubbed his hands together with anticipation. The subject of his curiosity was a man named Christian Fuller. Christian, a middle-aged, former auto mechanic from Bisbee, was quarantined in the garden section while they waited to see if, and when, he would turn. He had been bitten two days earlier when they were clearing the

Sonic parking lot a few blocks over. Christian had been in the process of putting down a family of zombies in an old Chevy Suburban with Sonora plates when a zombie crawled out from underneath and took a bite out of his calf. Knowing it was an instant death sentence, he had hid his wound from the rest of his unit, returning to his trailer as if nothing had happened. It was only blind luck that his roommate had caught a glimpse of the bite as Christian was dressing the next morning. Twelve hours had passed by that point, and he still showed no signs of infection. That was highly unusual.

Once his roommate raised the alarm, it was up to Pollard to decide what to do with Christian. His first impulse was to take him out back and put a bullet in his head. Just because. But he was curious. Bites typically resulted in death within an hour or two, and reanimation shortly thereafter. He had decided to wait and see what happened.

Pollard gestured at the door. "Keys?"

"Yes, sir," the teen responded. He pulled the keys from his pocket and tossed them over.

Pollard approached the gate on full alert. There was no sound from within. Putting his face up to the thick wire mesh, he scanned the cavernous space, searching for Christian. Dead plants. Enormous ceramic pots. Piles of tools. There was no sign of his quarry.

He rattled the gate. There was a low growl from beyond, and he instinctively took a step back. "Fuck!" Christian had turned.

Pollard pointed at Woo. "We need to talk. But first, we're going in there to check on him."

Woo's eyes grew wide. "In there?"

Pollard straightened and rested his hand on the butt of his pistol. He dropped his voice an octave. "Do you have a problem with that, son?"

Woo stole a glance at Steve, and then returned his attention to Pollard. "No, sir. Not at all, Mr. Pollard."

All morning Pollard had been mulling ways to test the boy. Feeding him to Hollister was a no-win situation for both him and Woo. She would screw him senseless for a week, maybe two, and then tire of him, at which point she would have him shot.

They would toss his corpse into the desert and leave him for the coyotes. He couldn't let that happen. This was a chance to get someone he trusted inside Hollister's room to learn just what the hell she was doing, to get a shot at taking her place. But first he had to let the kid in on his plan.

He had long ago abandoned the idea of challenging Hollister directly. As a submarine commander, she had done an adequate job. She was a little harsh on the crew, Pollard thought, but that was to be expected since she was the only woman on an all-male boat.

Ever since reaching land, though, she had changed into something he didn't recognize, as if her sense of right and wrong had been obliterated along with the cities destroyed by her missiles. Something inside had snapped, or maybe it had snapped earlier, and he had missed it. The more Pollard considered her behavior, the more he realized she may have been flawed from the very beginning. That, unfortunately, made him flawed by association. He couldn't live with it.

He hoped God, if he still existed, could forgive him for what he had done so far, and especially for what he was about to do in the name of setting things right.

"Weapons ready," he ordered, drawing his own pistol. Woo raised his rifle, a Browning .30-06, to his shoulder. Steve raised a wicked-looking double-barreled shotgun.

Pollard inserted the key into the lock and turned it slowly. It *clunked* as the bolt slid free. Through the mesh, he caught a flash of color and heard footsteps as Christian scampered through the space. Pollard held his breath for a second. The zombie, if that's what Christian was now, wasn't charging the door. *Very strange.*

"Cover me," he said, pulling the gate open just enough to slip through. Woo and Steve followed close behind.

"Lock it," Pollard said once they were all inside. Woo did. In front of them, a pair of check-out lanes flanked by more gates created a single point of entry into the dead store. Just beyond, brown, wilted plants cluttered the tables and benches to the far wall. A few cacti here and there had survived, splotches of dusky green in a vast sea of dingy brown. Pollard eyed the plants. *At least they don't come back. If they do, we may as well lie down and die.*

He called out, "Christian?" Nothing. He did it again, with more conviction in his voice. "Christian? It's Andrew Pollard. I've come to talk to you." Silence.

"He's in here somewhere," Steve whispered. "I saw him."

Pollard glared at him. "Quiet!" He took a few steps forward, past the end of the registers. Peered around the corner. All clear. *Shit. Where the hell did he go?*

He heard a crunching sound coming from behind a pallet of mulch. Woo's eyes grew wide. Pollard pointed at him and motioned to the left. He sent Steve to the right. He put his finger to his lips. Held their eyes until he was sure they understood. He put his finger on the trigger and made for the pallet. Woo followed.

Pollard thought he was ready for what he would find on the other side, but he couldn't have been more wrong. Christian, a thin and dirty man, was squatting behind the mulch, vigorously slurping the marrow from a splintered femur. He gagged, then choked it back. The femur was from a week-old undead he himself had executed. A morbid grin stretched across his face. *I was right! They do eat each other.*

He had suspected this for a while—that if the undead couldn't find a live food source, they would turn on each other, but he hadn't seen it in person. Not until today. His first hint had come when he and Hollister were in Northern Mexico. Somehow they had ended up at the tail-end of a long, snaking column of undead traveling in the same general direction. They hung back a safe distance, pacing the zombies, figuring that knowing where they were, and where they were headed, was far more valuable than hurrying to their destination.

Over the course of several days they had encountered numerous corpses that had been picked clean, bones cracked open like discarded sunflower shells, everything consumed but hair and teeth. None of it made sense. Zombies almost always left enough behind to reanimate. But that time, they hadn't.

He was walking point a few nights later when Hollister had suddenly grabbed his arm and hissed at him to stop *right now*. She had saved his life. Less than a hundred meters ahead was a small cluster of ghouls. Through the gloom, he and Hollister watched in mute horror as the creatures feasted on someone, wolfing down bits of flesh, tearing at the unlucky soul like a pack of starving hyenas. He couldn't make it out at the time, but Pollard swore the victim looked a little too ragged to be a living human. *And besides,* he had thought, *how would an uninfected wind up in the middle of a swarm this large?*

It hadn't added up at the time, but now it made perfect sense. They were cannibals. *On top of everything else.*

Christian eyed them each in turn, a low growl building in his throat. The femur shard clattered to the ground as he rose. Pollard's gut churned. He hated being this close to the undead. The stench made him ill. Worse than that was the knowledge that they were once people just like him. Sometimes he imagined they even looked like people he knew. Every time he killed one, he gave a silent apology.

"Ready?" he asked. Steve shifted to the right a foot, boxing Christian in. In a sudden moment of clarity, Pollard realized that if Steve shot from his current position, there was a good chance Christian's blood would spray all over himself and Woo, possibly infecting them.

"Steve!" he yelled. "We're in your line of fire! Move!" Anger surged through him. His pulse quickened. *He should know better.* Steve didn't move. He watched Christian, his eyes like a deer in the headlights. His finger slipped around the trigger.

Pollard nudged Woo with his elbow and nodded at Steve. "Shoot him."

"Huh?" Woo said, shifting his attention away from Christian.

"You heard me. Shoot him."

Christian opened his mouth. A moan was percolating deep in the back of his throat.

Steve's aim wavered. "What the fuck, Pollard?"

With a last uncertain glance, Woo swiveled his aim to Steve and pulled the trigger. Steve spun around as if grabbed from behind, crashed to the floor, and tumbled from view behind a stack of gravel.

Fresh meat. That was all the invitation Christian needed. He dove on Steve with a roar. Steve screamed and thrashed, his feet kicking wildly against the concrete floor. *He's still alive,* Pollard realized, sickened. Pollard and Woo watched and waited as Steve struggled with Christian, a losing battle to fight off the creature as it tried to consume him. It didn't take long. Soon the sounds of Steve's protests were replaced by the obscene cacophony of teeth rending flesh. Bits of gristle and blood flew indiscriminately, splattering the concrete.

Woo was shaking, the barrel of his gun jittering in crazy figure eights.

Pollard sighed. "Ok. I think that's enough." Woo gave him a blank look.

"That was a good shot," Pollard said, clapping him on the shoulder. He took a step forward and fired two shots into Christian's head. The zombie crumpled onto Steve's chest.

Sorry, Steve. He put three bullets into Steve's face, enough to guarantee he wouldn't get up again. "Don't worry," Pollard said as he turned back to Woo. "You passed the test."

Woo finally lowered his gun. "The test?" he asked incredulously. "What are you talking about?"

Pollard grinned and motioned at the exit. "Walk with me. I'll explain everything."

Twenty-One

They set out in a small convoy the next morning with four diesel pickup trucks liberated from the National Park Service depot adjacent to the Scorpion Canyon Ranger Station. Megan rode in the lead vehicle with Cesar, while Pringle followed in the next truck with Alicia. Four other men occupied the other vehicles bringing up the rear. Fuel wasn't a problem, at least for the foreseeable future. Diesel kept well, and the buried tank in the depot contained at least 5000 gallons. Beyond the ranger station, there were plenty of other sources of fuel if they ever ran out—enough to last a lifetime. *Or until the undead learned to drive.*

Today's raid was focused on food and medical supplies. The number of intact grocery stores had surprised them at first. Canned food was abundant, and it was only a matter of choosing what they wanted to haul back. Next week, Cesar planned to venture deeper into town to search for a rumored hydroponics supply store near the university, in hopes of setting up a sustainable indoor farming operation so they would have fresh produce during the long hot months.

So far, water wasn't a problem, either. While the river in the canyon was low at the moment, it provided plenty for the meager needs of the community. Still, Megan had her eyes open for some sort of cistern they could use to store water in case of a drought. She figured they could find one at a farm supply store.

They passed dozens of desiccated corpses as they picked their way through the remains of the city. They were true dead, detritus of the initial swarm that had surged through the city consuming everything in their path.

So far, the undead were nowhere to be seen. But that didn't mean they weren't there. It just meant they hadn't detected the convoy's presence yet. This worried Megan more than she let on.

Cesar slowed the truck and wove through the intersection of Speedway and Kolb, taking care not to get hung up on the wreckage of a black-and-white police cruiser and a crumpled BMW sport utility vehicle. As they cleared the wreck, Megan realized she was grinding her teeth. She took a deep breath and forced herself to relax. Being outside the fence always did this to her. She glanced out at the side-view mirror, searching for the chase vehicles.

One.

Two.

Her heart skipped a beat. *Where's the third?* A moment later the truck rumbled into view, swinging wide around the front bumper of the police cruiser. She let out a sigh of relief. The traffic, as packed as it was, offered far too many places for the undead to hide. They were like a live wire in the brush, lurking until someone disturbed them, instantly lethal.

"What the—" Cesar blurted. He stood on the brakes, and the truck jerked to a stop in the center of the road. Megan looked ahead and immediately saw the object of his concern. About a quarter of a mile down the road, there was a solitary figure facing them while sitting astride a motorcycle. The rider was clad from neck to toe in black leathers and wore a shiny black helmet with a smoked visor. It was definitely a man. Though it was impossible to see his face, his broad shoulders and narrow waist left little room for question.

A thousand thoughts raced through Megan's mind, but the one that set her heart racing was the possibility that they had driven into a trap. She had heard stories from other survivors in the compound and had even seen hints of it herself during her own journey south. Humanity had been reduced to interacting like dogs—bite first and make friends later.

The yellow Motorola radio on the dash squawked. "What's going on up there?"

Megan answered. "There's someone ahead. We don't know if he's friendly."

Silence for a second, and then, "I can't see him."

"He's on a motorcycle." Megan watched Cesar's face, trying to gauge his reaction to the situation. He looked lost in thought, hands at ten and two on the wheel, thumbs drumming as he pondered their options.

"Hold on, Mike," Megan said into the radio handset.

The man climbed from his bike and put out his kickstand. He took a step away and checked his surroundings. He started to remove his helmet.

"I don't see any weapons," Megan whispered. "What do you think, Cesar?"

He shrugged and pulled a pair of binoculars from the door pocket to scan the area. "I don't see anyone else." He scanned behind them. "We go forward," he finally said, removing his foot from the brake.

As they got within twenty feet of the motorcyclist, Megan was finally able to make out part of his face through the shadow of his helmet. Still, she couldn't shake the feeling they were driving into some sort of ambush. She craned her head around and scanned the buildings lining the road, searching for anything out of the ordinary.

Ten feet from the motorcycle, Cesar rolled to a stop and threw the truck in park. "Stay here," he said.

"Not a chance." Megan grabbed her pistol and reached for the door latch.

Cesar grabbed her forearm, his grip like a vise. "I need you here Megan. Just in case." He gestured at the man with his other hand. "I want you to get behind the wheel and be ready to go." The look in his eyes said he wouldn't take no for an answer.

"Okay," she agreed. "But I don't like it." She cast her eyes down at his hand still gripping her forearm.

He released her. "I'm sorry…"

"Don't worry about it." She picked up the radio and told the other vehicles to hold their positions. Cesar exited the truck and walked briskly toward the man. Megan slid behind the wheel and placed her pistol on the dashboard. Just in case.

The motorcycle guy looked a little rough, like he'd been on the road for a long time. Dirt caked his face, and fine lines crinkled at the corners of his eyes as he squinted into the sun. His short blond hair looked greasy, as if it hadn't been washed in ages. Megan couldn't hear their discussion over the rumble of the engine, but their body language looked promising.

After a minute, Cesar turned and gestured at the convoy. The man said something with a smile and pointed north. She guessed that was where he had come from. They exchanged a few more words, shook hands, and began walking toward the truck. Megan took the gun off the dash and put it in her lap with the barrel pointed at the door. She straightened in her seat and waited.

Cesar and the man arrived at her window. "Megan, I'd like you to meet Kevin…" Cesar stumbled, obviously having forgotten the man's last name already.

"Salerno," the stranger interjected. His voice was deep and full of confidence, and Megan had a sudden intuition he had seen a lot in whatever life he had led before the end of the world. "Nice to meet you," he said, offering his hand.

"Likewise." Megan stuck her hand out the window, and they shook.

"Kevin's been on the road for a while," Cesar added. Megan noted the desperate hunger in Kevin's eyes. *He's searching for something.*

Cesar pressed on. "He's going to stay with us for a few days. Maybe more."

Megan's mind raced as she considered where Kevin would fit into the community. There was no doubt he was road-hardened. He knew how to drive a bike, perfect for getting through tight traffic situations. *Maybe a scout?*

"I told him about our scavenging operation. He's going to help today, and then follow us back afterward."

"Sounds good." Actually, it was great, the more people on a raid, the better their chances of success.

"Not many undead around here today, are there?" Kevin commented, inclining his head in Megan's direction. "But it looks like you guys are loaded for bear."

"Oh, they're here," Cesar responded. He glanced nervously at the surrounding buildings. "I don't know where yet, but they're here." There was a lull in the conversation as they all evaluated their new situation.

Cesar spoke first. "Fall in somewhere in the middle, Kevin. Follow our lead for now, and you'll be all right."

"That works." Kevin pulled on his helmet and turned for his motorcycle. He fired it up and cut a wide circle around the group, placing himself in the middle, just behind Pringle. He sat and idled, waiting for the convoy to lurch forward. By the time Cesar had situated himself behind the wheel, Megan had already briefed the others in the convoy, including Pringle, who seemed oddly ambivalent about the new addition.

They set off. They still had supplies to collect.

Twenty-Two

Albuquerque as Jack had known it no longer existed. The only thing left was the blackened stumps of buildings and charred earth as far as he could see. Ash and drifts of fine dust clung to every surface, turning the environment a muted, monochromatic gray. The pervasive stench of death blotted out the once fragrant scent of the high desert. Even the Sandia Mountains hadn't escaped the devastation. Every tree on the west-facing slope had been burned away, allowing the late-summer rains to scour the denuded hillside, sloughing millions of tons of dirt and rock into the city below. Zombies ruled the countryside. They were everywhere, preserved for all eternity by the great clouds of radiation roiling in the atmosphere.

It was colder than usual, probably ten or fifteen degrees below normal. This was because of the bombs; the dust they had kicked up was blocking the sun's rays from reaching the earth, cooling the northern hemisphere in a vicious feedback loop that Jack knew wouldn't end until all of the dust settled. And that could be years.

So they headed south.

It was the only way to survive. He had no idea how far he would have to go to reach a warmer climate, or if the radiation would get them first. He worried about poisonous clouds from southern California and Arizona sweeping over them, but there was little he could do. They had to go south, or they would die.

The terrifying truth was that with civilization gone, Jack and Becka were going to have to learn how to produce their own food. Scavenging would only take them so far; canned goods would last a few years at best, maybe more, but they weren't the answer to long-term survival. No, to really make it, they had to become modern-day farmers, and the New Mexico high country wasn't the place for that. not anymore.

He had to laugh at the irony of it all. Before the world collapsed, there had been whole magazines—hell, whole *industries*—devoted to the idealized notion of getting back to nature, of being self-sufficient. He knew this because he had a stack of those very magazines, complete with glossy full page advertisements for fancy micro-tractors and do-it-yourself solar water heaters, in his bathroom back in Taos.

Jack wiped his brow with his sleeve, scrubbing away a thick rivulet of sweat before it ran into his eyes.

"Are we there yet?" Ellie called out from the rear seat of their ancient Volkswagen camper. "Can we stop for nuggets soon?" Jack opened his mouth to answer, but found he couldn't make the words come out. A tear leaked from his eye. He wiped it away. Ellie's question had struck a chord deep inside of him, triggering a flood of memories of better times.

Becka came to his rescue. "No, honey. Not yet."

Their vehicle was remarkably well-preserved considering it was over a half-century old. There wasn't a spot of rust on the body, and the engine, clattering and pinging like a sewing machine on steroids, ran like a champ. Finding the pre-electronic-ignition camper on the side of I-25 north of Albuquerque had been a stroke of unbelievable luck, for while he and Becka could walk for days, Ellie was another story. She could only put in six or seven miles on a good day, not nearly enough to get them to their destination, wherever that was. White with broad maroon racing stripes on each side, the camper was immaculate except for a large, dried bloodstain saturating the driver's seat. Jack had no idea if the blood was infectious, and he wasn't taking any chances. A blue tarp, liberated from a storage compartment in the rear, solved this problem in short order. Now he just had to deal with the constant crinkling as he shifted around. The sound drove him crazy.

They were running along at fifty miles per hour, having just cleared the southern edge of Albuquerque, when things turned to shit. Out of the corner of his eye, he saw a yellow and black sign announcing they were entering open-range country. That meant the cattle were not behind fences; they were free to move across the road at any time of day or night.

He recalled a trip many years earlier, before Maddie and Ellie were born. He and Becka had been on their way to Denver to visit some college friends. It was early in the morning, just after sunrise, and they had been driving all night, pushing north through a late-spring snowstorm. Becka had spotted it first, as they crested a sharp rise about a hundred miles south of the Colorado border. "What's that?" she asked, pointing at the road ahead. Jack leaned forward and squinted through the snow, trying to make sense of what he was seeing. It looked like a load of trash had escaped the bed of a pickup truck, but worse. Both northbound lanes were littered with snow-covered obstructions. He lifted his foot from the gas, allowing the car to slow on its own.

Becka's eyes grew wide. "Oh, my God, Jack! That's an accident!"

They had come to a stop a few feet away from the remains of a horrific collision between some sort of livestock, probably a cow, and a small car. The car appeared to be a Honda Civic or Toyota Tercel, but they couldn't tell for sure. Whatever it had been, no amount of repairs would ever make it whole again.

There was nothing left of the driver larger than a child's lunch box.

"Call 911," Jack whispered.

Becka had retrieved her phone from her purse and punched in the numbers. A moment later, she frowned and held it out to him. "No signal."

Jack cursed. That was in the days before the mobile phone companies finished expanding their networks, when it was still possible to get lost in the great empty spaces between the cities of the mountain west. It had taken them over an hour to reach an area with enough cellular reception to report the accident.

The tragedy had been covered in the Denver Post the next morning. The driver, a man of about Jack's age, had been on his way back from a family reunion in Las Vegas, New Mexico, when he fell asleep at the wheel and encountered a stray cow shortly after midnight.

Jack swallowed the memory away. *If that happened now, if we were to hit an animal or if we were to hit anything, there would be no one to call for help...* He let out a nervous laugh. *It's just a sign,* he told himself. *It doesn't mean anything anymore.*

Something moved on the side of the road.

"Hold on!" He tensed up. He didn't have time to put his hand out to stabilize Becka before the creature darted into their path. It was a runner, one of the irradiated ones from Albuquerque, and it was moving fast, almost sprinting.

A man. One arm. No skin on the side of his head. These images were burned into Jack's mind as the creature plunged into the scrub on the opposite side of the road. He feathered the brake. *The undead never traveled alone.* He was right. A second creature appeared as if summoned, and raced into his lane. Jack swerved, but not enough.

The second zombie plowed into the right front corner of the bus, causing its body to explode into a greasy mist of gore. The old VW shuddered and jumped left a few inches as the steering wheel was torn from his grasp. He gripped the wheel and tried to bring it back to straighten the bus. *Bang!* They slewed violently to the right. *Tire!*

Jack put every ounce of strength he possessed into straightening the van, but the top-heavy vehicle had its own plans. Time slowed. He felt the tires on the left side of the bus lose contact with the road. They went airborne. A second later, the earth reached up and yanked them back in a vicious embrace. Glass exploded around him in a million glittering fragments. Twisting metal screamed in his ears. Hot sparks peppered his face, minute pinpricks of heat that felt oddly comforting.

And then everything went black.

~~~

Consciousness seeped into Jack's mind with agonizing slowness. The first thing he noticed was the temperature. It was much colder, almost freezing. He was shivering, his entire body quaking uncontrollably. He tried to move. He couldn't. His hips felt torn, as if some enormous creature had taken hold of either side of his body and wrung him like dish rag. He tried to open his eyes but his lids wouldn't budge. Glued shut.

"What the hell…?" His head pounded. Blood thrummed in his ears, the rushing boom boom drowning out everything around him. Stretching the muscles of his face, he finally managed to open his eyes. He let out a surprised cry. The world was upside down. No. Wait. He was upside down.

The pain in his hips was from the lap belt digging into his waist and cutting off his circulation. He hung there for a moment and stared. With his right hand, Jack felt for the roof and discovered it was only an inch from the top of his head. Windshield glass lay scattered below, tiny stars twinkling at him from a false night sky.

He groaned. His head was thick, full of itchy wool. His mind tripped over itself, trying to piece together the events that had put him here. It all came back in a terrifying gut-wrenching rush.

"Becka! Ellie!" he shouted. He twisted in his seat, searching for them. Becka wasn't there. He couldn't turn far enough to see into the rear. "Becka! Ellie!" he called again.

As he twisted, a lance of pain raced up his arm and into his shoulder, flooding his mind with an agony beyond any he had ever experienced. Bile tumbled down his throat and dribbled onto the roof of his mouth. He vomited an explosive torrent of steaming fluid that gushed back into his upturned nose, choking him.
~~~

Looking at his arm, he discovered the source of the pain, a jagged shard of glass, embedded in the meaty part of his upper bicep. Protruding at an obscene angle, the glass was lodged deep inside the muscle, grinding against bone every time he moved. His vision went gray around the edges. He realized he was about to black out. He fought it, wrapping his mind around the wispy tendrils of consciousness as they sprinted away from him, reeling them back in and gathering them close.

Becka. Ellie. Got to find them. Gritting his teeth, Jack grasped the shard with his good hand and tugged with all his might. He couldn't hold back a scream as the glass slid free. Blood welled up from the wound, then splattered on the roof of the van. Reaching for the belt buckle with his good arm, he took a deep breath and pressed the release.

Although he didn't have far to fall, the impact still knocked the wind out of him. It seemed as if every square inch of his body had been pummeled during the accident. He lay still for a moment, panting, trying his best not to black out again. Free from his bonds, Jack rolled over and began searching for his family.

They were gone. He crawled to the front passenger seat and took Becka's seat belt in his hand. Panic welled up as he fingered the ends of the straps. They were torn and shredded, as if something had gnawed through them.

He crawled into the back. It was empty as well. The windows had all imploded, compressed beyond their engineering limits when the bus landed on its roof. A chill desert breeze flowed through the empty frames. He flicked the switch on the dome lamp between his knees. *Dead.*

His stomach sank. Blood coated every surface, congealing pools soaking through the knees of his jeans and coating his hands as he turned in frantic circles.

Zombies. He sat back on his haunches to consider the situation. *This doesn't make sense. If zombies took them, then why am I still here? Why didn't they take me, too?*

Maybe they had been ejected from the bus as it rolled. Jack's hopes soared. But no. That wouldn't explain Becka's seat belt. Or the blood in the rear. Ellie's blood. Hell, he couldn't even remember if Ellie had even been buckled in. *Probably not.* She hated seat belts.

Jack kicked open the door and crawled onto the desert floor. The sand was cool under his palms. The moon rode high overhead. *Midnight, maybe later. I wasn't out for long.* A wave of nausea assaulted him as he struggled to his feet. He put his hands on his knees to stabilize himself and retched, burping up foul acid. He spit.

Mangled beyond repair, the bus lay at the bottom of a shallow wash. Their supplies, ejected during the crash, charted their unexpected departure from the freeway like a trail of enormous breadcrumbs. There was a sleeping bag at his feet, and their Coleman stove lay a few yards beyond. He found his pistol half-buried in the sand a few feet from the bus.

But no Becka. And no Ellie.

Jack scrambled up the embankment, the loose sand crumbling beneath his fingers with each frantic grasp. Finally, he made it to the top. The remains of the ghoul he had hit twitched mindlessly on the shoulder, his muscles contracting and releasing like some mad perpetual-motion machine. Now that his eyes were adjusted to the dark, he realized he could see for miles. The desert glowed as if lit from within.

Jack cupped his hand around his mouth and yelled. "Becka! Ellie!" He listened. Seconds ticked by with no response. Crossing the road, he repeated his call. He waited again. Nothing.

Something *snapped* behind him. Something brittle. Near the bus. Jack sprinted across the road to the lip of the arroyo and peered in. A ripping sound, like Velcro, split the silence.

Jack's hopes soared. "Becka?" There was no answer. Jack plunged down the embankment, imagining Becka with a life-threatening injury, unable to answer.

"Becka! Ellie!" he shouted as he dashed around the bus. There was no one there. Jack skidded to a stop. He looked around, puzzled. *Where's it coming from?*

His answer came a moment later, when another, louder ripping sound split the night air. It was coming from a few dozen yards farther down the wash, near the corpse of a monstrous cottonwood.

He checked his weapon, ensuring the safety was off. "Becka?" he said in a low voice. "I'm coming..." As quietly as he could, Jack made his way through the arroyo. His heart raced and sweat poured from his forehead despite the cool breeze.

He approached the tree. How a tree this large had been torn loose baffled him. It was easily three feet across, with bleached-white limbs stretching towards the night sky like a spurned lover.

"Becka?" The ripping sound came again. Something moved just a few feet in front of him. Despite the moonlight, Jack wished he had a flashlight. He couldn't make out any shapes through the jumble of shadows. He stepped forward.

From beneath a tangle of branches, Becka stared up at him, a rictus of agony stretched across her face.

"Ellie. No."

Ellie was crouched to one side, chewing vigorously on her mother's limp arm. At the sound of his voice, her head snapped up, and she locked eyes with Jack, the milky-whites seeming to penetrate to the bottom of his soul. Jack took a step back and raised his hands, his gun pointing at the sky.

Ellie leaped to her feet. She growled. Becka didn't move.

Jack swallowed. Cold washed through his body. He shivered uncontrollably. His teeth began to chatter, causing him to nick his tongue, sending a flood of coppery-tasting blood into his mouth. He swallowed hard.

Ellie stepped over her mother and began lumbering toward him. One leg was obviously broken, twisted and shattered into a useless sack of bone and flesh. Yet, she still came.

Jack centered his pistol on her forehead. And then he pulled the trigger. The shot hit home, and Ellie collapsed to the ground. Silence returned. But he wasn't done. Becka *would* rise as well. Maybe in minutes, maybe in hours, but she would come back.

Jack made his way to his wife's body. He kneeled down beside her and touched her left cheek. It was still warm. He tasted metal in the back of his throat. Cold and antiseptic, bitter. Almost oily. With a quick swipe of his thumb and index finger, he closed Becka's eyelids. He put his pistol against her forehead.

"I'm sorry, honey."

He pulled the trigger.

Twenty-Three

The parking lot was empty. Or, more accurately, it *appeared* empty. Megan scanned the storefronts one by one, plumbing the depths of the dark shops lining the strip mall, wishing she could see through the walls to spy the creatures that surely lurked within. The whole day had been this way, with very little undead presence to speak of. That bothered her. Typically, when you didn't see them coming was when they would pop out of a dark corner and take a chunk out of your ass. She had seen it firsthand, had almost been dinner herself on more than one occasion.

Something about this food raid was making her jumpy, like she felt when she had left the house and forgotten to turn off the oven. She turned to Cesar. "Do you—"

Cesar shushed her. "I know. I feel it too. Something's off..." She looked over her shoulder at the new guy, Kevin. He was going car to car, checking for trapped ghouls and ensuring the doors were locked. *He's thorough,* she decided.

It was silent in the grocery store parking lot, since all of the engines were stopped. That was often the worst part. The sounds of the heavy diesel engines would sometimes bring the undead out en masse, forcing them to abandon a raid. She and Cesar had experimented with using a decoy vehicle, sending it ahead to pull out the lurking ghouls and lead them away, but it seemed that no matter how many were collected, there were always more left behind.

"Mo, you and Rich," Cesar said, addressing the drivers of the chase vehicles. "I want you guys out here." He turned to Kevin. "You, too. We'll be quick."

The men nodded in agreement and set up positions on either side of the entrance with their weapons pointing out.

Entering an abandoned building was one of Megan's least favorite activities. Together, she, Cesar, and Pringle forced the front door as quietly as possible and crept inside. Despite the brilliant daylight only a few feet behind them, her eyes couldn't penetrate the gloom of the interior.

"Fuck," she whispered under her breath.

"Yes. Fuck," Cesar agreed. Cesar wasn't given to cursing, even in the most difficult situation, and that one word told her volumes about how he felt.

"Are you sure you want to do this?" she asked.

"*Sí*. Yes. The next one is three miles to the South. I don't want to go that far into town. Not today."

"Okay then." Megan took a deep breath. "Let's get this over with." Hauling her arm back, she lobbed a fist-sized rock deep into the store.

The response was immediate. A cacophony of moans, the call of the undead.

"Come to Mama," she said under her breath. One of the creatures came blundering into her vision, getting hung up on an overturned shopping cart for a moment before knocking it aside and vectoring straight toward her position. It looked to have been a soccer mom in its former life. Thirty-something with a cute pair of yoga pants and nearly new running shoes, she was perfectly preserved except for the gaping cavity in her abdomen where all of the internal organs were supposed to be. The soccer mom staggered between a set of cash registers, bumbling and tripping, spinning around in its desperate rush to reach food.

Megan felt the muscles in her neck tense, her jaw ached and her teeth ground relentlessly. She flexed her fingers and forced herself to breathe, to relax. She hefted her mattock, taking comfort at its solidity. At a little over five-feet-long, the device was one of Cesar's finest creations, a cross between a shovel handle and a traditional mattock. Quick, quiet, and deadly effective at close range, it was the most practical way to dispatch the undead without the siren song of gunshots. Cesar had come up with the idea after a harrowing raid in which they had accidentally attracted half of Tucson's undead. The blade of the mattock was perfect for slowing them down, removing limbs, and chopping them off at the knees. The spike was custom-built for the head. It was large and heavy enough to penetrate all but the thickest of skulls, able to drop a zombie with a single strike.

Cesar carried a similar weapon, although a slightly beefier version. They also carried pistols in case they were overrun. Everyone carried one extra bullet, just in case. The guns were a last resort. Firing a shot was akin to ringing the dinner bell.

As the soccer mom drew closer, she raised her hands like a baby seeking its mother and ground her teeth. She raced at Megan, a flesh-seeking missile full of deadly intent. Megan stepped to the side at the last second, removing herself from the woman's direct path. Cesar stood ready to assist. The creature was slow to react, and by the time it realized dinner had moved, Megan was behind it, bringing her spike into its skull with a satisfying crunch.

They took extra care to sterilize their weapons at the end of each engagement. As far as they could tell, the two surefire ways to get infected were to be bitten or to get infected brain matter into an open cut, or in an eye.

"Nice!" Cesar said. Megan couldn't help feeling a flush of pride at her handiwork. There was more shuffling from the aisles beyond the registers. More moaning.

"Inbound," Pringle said through clenched teeth.

Next up were two young boys, no more than ten years old. They were faster than the woman, dashing out of the coffee aisle, pausing briefly to fixate on the raiding team, and then scrambling forward. Cesar held up two fingers. He pointed once to the right and once to the left. Then he swiped them straight ahead. A kill box. Megan and Pringle were to funnel the creatures into the center where they could concentrate their efforts. They used the ends of their poles to force the ghouls together, and then with a flash of their blades, sliced the tendons behind their knees. The creatures tumbled to the ground and began thrashing in frustration. With a stern look, Pringle stepped forward and smashed both diseased heads with his aluminum baseball bat, pulping both skulls on the dirty linoleum floor.

They all paused to catch their breath. Aside from Pringle's wheezing, the store was silent. No more moans. No more undead.

"Here, zombie, zombie," Pringle chanted, like the child he had just destroyed might have before he had been turned. "Come and get us."

Cesar gave him a wry grin.

"Cesar?" Kevin sounded alarmed. Cesar held up his hand, motioning for him to wait.

"We've got company," Kevin insisted, the urgency in his voice unmistakable. That changed everything. Megan spun around and dashed through the front door.

Undead were swarming the parking lot, filtering through abandoned cars by the dozens. More were arriving by the second from all directions. Megan's bowels turned to water. Her pulse skyrocketed. "Cesar?" She croaked.

This was their worst nightmare. This was how the best-laid plans became suicide missions. It was all in the numbers. Fighting one undead was easy. Pop it in the head and down it went. Fighting two was a bit more of a challenge; it could even be fun if you had the right mindset. Fighting dozens, and she noticed even more coming around the northwestern corner, was damned near impossible. They never gave up, never retreated. Their manual weapons lost almost all of their effectiveness when faced with more than three or four. It was time to bring out the guns.

But guns were only so effective. It required a perfect headshot to drop a zombie, and this became exponentially more difficult when they encountered a runner. Up to about three or four meters, Megan could make the kill every time. Beyond that, her accuracy fell off a cliff. And she wasn't alone.

Cesar looked over his shoulder into the maw of the store and then back out to the rapidly-filling parking lot. "We're leaving right now," he announced. "Everybody out! Go! Go! Go!"

They scattered for their vehicles. By this point, zombies were everywhere, blocking the exits, a seething mass of flesh-hungry monsters with one thing on their mind: Dinner.

The truck roared as Cesar swung around looking for space to build up some speed. They were going to have to drive through the crowd, Megan realized with a sinking feeling. Kevin was straddling his motorcycle when one of the creatures reached for his shoulder. Megan watched in awe as he ducked down, drew his shotgun and placed it against the creature's face. Its head disappeared into a gray-black mist, and the corpse tumbled away. Kevin re-holstered his gun, and ducking and weaving as he searched for a way out, he sped off through the mass of creatures.

"Here we go," Cesar growled. He punched the accelerator. and the tires squealed in protest. Megan pushed back in her seat, grabbing the armrest with one hand and her pistol with the other. The first couple of undead went down with no problem, bouncing off the hood and tumbling to the side. Then, suddenly, in front of them was a dense cluster moving as one toward the truck.

"Hold on!" Cesar screamed over the roar of the engine, then he plowed straight into them. There was an enormous *crash*, and before she knew what was happening, the windshield was gone, and one of the things was in her lap. It thrashed wildly, its fetid stink choking her with every breath.

"Get it off of me!" Megan screamed, disgusted at the feel of rotten skin sloughing off as the creature sought purchase on her body. Cesar swerved back and forth, shaking the other creatures loose from the hood, finally finding a gap. They were out of the crowd, and except for the ghoul in the cab with them, they had a clear shot at the road. Megan was frozen in place, watching in detached horror as the creature in her lap tried to bite into her leg.

Formerly a large man in his thirties, the lack of arms, probably torn off during the impact with the truck, made him look like a fat mutant snake as he writhed around in her lap. It was only a matter of time before he got lucky and sank his teeth into her flesh. In a fit of panic, Megan placed her gun against the man's temple, turned her head away, and fired a single shot. The report obliterated her hearing, turning everything to a low rush of muffled white noise. Cordite permeated the cab for a moment before it was washed away by the wind.

Cesar slammed on the brakes, and they skidded to a stop in the center of the southbound lane. Megan leaped from the truck, and hauled the corpse out by its feet, dumping it unceremoniously on the side of the road.

Then, as she climbed back into the truck, her heart nearly stopped. The entire side of Cesar's face was covered in a sticky, black, syrupy-looking substance. Zombie brains. She felt herself go cold when she realized what had happened. Back-splatter.

Cesar blinked, put the truck back in gear and started rolling as soon as she was back inside.

"Oh, my God!" She reached for him, but he shrank away, not letting her get the toxic sludge on her fingers.

He shook his head. "You did what you had to do."

"I didn't…"she stammered.

He laughed, a high pitched chitter she had never heard from him before. "*We* all have to go sometime, Megan." Megan's heart fell as the words sank in. Cesar didn't have much time, hours, at most. Probably less.

"Cesar. I'm so sorry," she said again and again, repeating it as he drove, as if somehow it would undo things. They drove for the next fifteen minutes, weaving through town in a careful circuit designed to throw the undead off of their trail to avoid bringing them to their doorstep. Once they lost sight of the horde, Cesar slowed the truck and pulled to the side of the road. He shifted into Park and left the engine running.

"What are you doing?" Megan asked, alarmed. "We're nowhere near home." She knew exactly what he was doing, but she didn't want to acknowledge it. Cesar didn't answer. Instead, he leaned forward and rested his chin on his hands which were still on the steering wheel. He stared out at the desert.

The radio squawked. "What's going on up there?"

Megan answered. "Nothing. Give us a minute." She threw the radio onto the dash. A bead of sweat trickled from beneath the brim of Cesar's hat. It rolled down the side of his face and vanished into the collar of his shirt.

"Cesar?" she asked tentatively.

"Megan," he answered slowly. "I've had a good life. Better than anyone..."

"No! You can't!"

He turned to face her with profound sadness blanketing his face. "I… We have no choice now. You know that." Megan shook her head, flinging hot tears from her face. Gravel crunched outside her window; instantly, she turned and raised her pistol.

Pringle took a step back, arms raised. "Easy there, Megan. You almost—"

"Mike. Now is not the time!" She turned back to Cesar. "There's got to be a way. Maybe you're not even infected."

"What's this about infection?" Pringle asked, suddenly serious. He opened the passenger door and leaned inside the truck.

"I got splattered. It got in my eye," Cesar replied without emotion. "I can feel it inside of me. It burns, deep down."

"Maybe you're imagining it?" She offered.

"No. I'm infected."

"Holy shit, Cesar," Pringle said. "How did it happen?"

Cesar glanced at Megan. "It doesn't matter now." There was a long pause as they all considered the ramifications. The truck rumbled, the engine clattering in the heat.

"I'd like to do it here," Cesar continued. "This is my home." Megan looked around. As far as places to die, she could think of a lot worse. They were on the outskirts of town, surrounded by low rolling hills studded with majestic saguaro, prickly pear, and cholla cacti. She bit back a sob.

"We can't do this without you, Cesar," she pleaded, sneaking a glance at Pringle.

"Yes, you can," Cesar replied calmly. "You have to." She opened her mouth to protest, but there were no more words. "You're strong, Megan, stronger than you know." He turned to Pringle. "And, Mike, you're a good man despite yourself." Pringle looked at the ground. "Megan, I want you to take over. You have to work together, to be strong, if you want this to succeed, if you want to survive..."

He was sweating more, his shirt growing damp. His skin was sallow, his breaths becoming shorter and shorter. He didn't have much time left. Cesar forced a smile.

"Why not Mike?" Megan asked.

"Yeah, why not?" Pringle whined. "I've been here as long as Megan. I know the people. I know everything."

Cesar shook his head. "Mike, you're great at what you do. And you need to keep doing it. Megan... she has a special gift with people. They listen to her. But she can't do it without you. Your role is essential to making this community work."

Pringle didn't respond for a long moment. Finally, he nodded, but something in his eyes told Megan this wasn't the end of the discussion.

Cesar looked them both in the eye. "Okay, then. That's settled." He opened the driver's side door and climbed from the truck. "I don't want to put either of you through the trauma of killing me, so I'll take care of it myself." Megan moved to hug him, an involuntary response, but Cesar took a step back. He was already gone.

He proceeded to strip off his extra ammunition, his boots, and his radio gear, placing it all in the bed of the truck. He ejected all of the ammunition from his pistol except one bullet, stacking the cartridges in a neat pile on the seat. With a final nod, he turned and strode into the desert, vanishing into the brush forever.

Megan sniffed, wiped her eyes, and moved across the bench seat, taking her place behind the wheel. "You getting in?" she asked Mike. "It sounds like we've got a lot to discuss."

Mike waved his arm at the other truck to let them know they could continue without him, and then climbed into the passenger seat.

With a last glance at the desert that had consumed Cesar, Megan put the truck back in gear and started driving north.

She couldn't stand to hear the shot.

Twenty-Four

Private First Class Jimmy LaTour put a finger over his left nostril and blew gooey chunks of dirt-infused snot on the dung-colored rocks at his feet. He jumped as a fast moving shadow flashed across the ground beside him. He looked up. It was only a hawk, riding a thermal on the hunt. For a second, Jimmy wished he was the bird, able to escape the bounds of earth and fly away. He chuckled at the thought.

The last time he had seen a plane was shortly after he had hooked up with Hollister's crew. It had been a momentary glint in the heavens, hurtling from east to west before it was swallowed up by the late-afternoon sun. Where it came from and who was flying it, he would never know. He had dutifully reported the sighting to his crew boss, and then promptly forgot about it.

Not that it mattered anymore. Jimmy had long ago abandoned the idea of anyone coming to his rescue. Hell, if the US Army couldn't even defend their own base, then what chance did anyone else have? He often wondered about the other soldiers in his unit, the men and women still in Afghanistan. Was it as bad over there? Were they still alive? Fortunately for him, he was on leave the day the world died, shacked up with his girlfriend Felecia in a cabin on Mount Lemmon. Felecia was gone now, dragged kicking and screaming from his pickup truck and dismembered before his eyes as they sat in a traffic jam at the main gate. Jimmy had managed to destroy the creatures eating her, but by then it was too late. He put two into her head as she began to claw her way towards him. From there, it was a frantic scramble on foot, ducking and weaving through the feeding frenzy and barely making it through the gate before it closed for good.

That hadn't lasted long either. By the time the night was out, the base was overrun, zombies swarming through every building, looking for fresh sustenance. Jimmy had hidden. Like a scared little boy, he locked himself inside a walk-in freezer in the mess hall. There he waited.

The first challenge was the cold. That was solved at the end of the third day when the generators failed. Then the heat became a problem, exacerbated by the suffocating stench of rotting food and his own waste. Finally, when he couldn't stand it anymore, when he reached the point where he figured it would be better to be eaten alive than to die like a trapped animal, he had ventured out. The zombies were gone.

Signs of the battle were everywhere, bits and pieces of corpses, morsels of discarded flesh, and pools of congealed blood. But no one else was alive, and no infected ones remained. He was alone.

Jimmy's first thought had been to find out what had happened to everyone, to see if anyone else was still alive. That was a dead-end. Without power, communications were no longer an option. Fortunately, the Army was still a largely paper-based organization, and Jimmy found, after a little searching in the base commander's office, a treasure trove of information about the final hours. What he read cemented his convictions that there was little chance of anyone else being alive.

The infection had come out of nowhere, sweeping across the globe in a matter of hours. The first cases were reported in Sydney, Australia, but that meant little, because within hours, the infection appeared in New York, London, Moscow, and then Los Angeles. The reports were rife with speculation as to the source. A biological weapon run amok? A naturally-occurring pathogen triggered by environmental factors? No one knew, and there was no time to figure it out. It moved too fast.

His final discovery was the most chilling. A set of orders from high in the Defense Department instructed the base commander to prepare for nuclear attack. The government was preparing to launch its entire arsenal of tactical and strategic nuclear weapons against domestic population centers in a last-ditch effort to eradicate the threat.

But that was then. Today, Jimmy was perched high above Tucson, on the southern end of the Rincon mountains, searching for other survivors. Ever since Hollister had rolled into town, his life had regained purpose. He shrugged off his pack, dropped it to his feet, and began to dig around in the top compartment. A moment later, he found what he was looking for. He pulled out a small nylon pouch and brought it to his lips, giving it a loving kiss.

From within, he extracted a green blown-glass pipe and a small plastic bag. He selected a bulbous crystal of methamphetamine and nestled it into the bowl. He struck his lighter and took a long, burning hit, drawing the vapors deep into the far recesses of his lungs. All of his synapses fired at once as the chemicals coursed through his blood stream, sending all thoughts of his old life away with the wind.

I wonder if the undead can get high? he mused, before dismissing it as ridiculous. They didn't seem to breathe as far as he could tell. Hell, some of them didn't even have lungs anymore. Where would the smoke go? He chuckled at the image of clouds of sweet smoke billowing from a hollowed-out chest cavity. He laughed again, the high-pitched titter of someone tweaking along the razor edge of sanity.

He took another hit, this time with his eyes open, and relished the sensation as the various shades of brown and muted green dotting the valley below snapped into focus. It was like watching an HD television beside an old piece-of-shit standard set. Reality held little interest for Jimmy at this point, and he was okay with that. Reality was for ordinary people, and he was anything but. He was a survivor, and he intended to keep right on surviving. But that all depended on how he performed in his new role as a scout. It was a big promotion from *body-burning.* Huge.

Body-burning. What a disgusting job. He used to laugh at vegetarians. Not anymore. He was done with meat. Never again.

That was life in Hollister's army. *Or whatever she was calling it today.* It was only a few hundred people so far, but it was growing fast. They were absorbing refugees from the countryside, people who had survived the initial collapse but were now running out of food and ammunition, people who needed someone to follow. That's why Jimmy was on the ridge; he was scouting Tucson for new recruits. From a safe distance, of course.

Before things went to shit, he had always said that the world was fucked up, that too many people got away with doing too little. Well, that sure wasn't the case anymore. If you didn't pull your weight in the new world, then you became zombie-chow. Fast.

Fuck. Tweaking hard. Can't focus. Jimmy realized it was time to get back to the business of why he had hiked halfway up this godforsaken mountain in the first place. Scouting. He took a quick sip from the water bottle strapped to his waist and then peeled open the bottom half of his pack, exposing a long-range spotter scope. He had practiced with it before leaving Sierra Vista, and he had it assembled and mounted on its tripod in under a minute.

The scope gave him a good view of east Tucson without having to go down into town and risk his ass. He unfolded a map and a small notebook and placed them on the ground beside the tripod. Rocks went on each corner to hold down the notebook.

His job today was simple: Scan this side of the city, the entry and exit points, and put together a summary of what he saw, zombie clusters, road blockages, likely supply sources, and whatever else caught his attention. There was another scout somewhere else on the mountain. He didn't know who, but he was sure their results would be compared when they returned. He wondered who it was. Hollister and Pollard were sneaky like that, always playing people against each other.

Stop. Gotta stop obsessing over this shit. The meth had a way of doing that. If he didn't concentrate, his thoughts would run away with themselves, and he wouldn't get the job done. Then he would be back to burning bodies. Or worse.

He counted backward from ten, settled down, and put his eye to the scope. He swiveled it north and started scanning. A few minutes later, he pulled back and yawned. *What a boring fucking job.* There was no way he could do it without the rock to help him focus. So far he had noted a handful of grocery stores still standing and at least one sizable cluster of undead stuck inside the chain-link fences of a city park. He checked his map. Lincoln Park. Baseball diamonds, soccer fields, and lots of fences to confuse the stupid bastards. Why the dumb fucks couldn't find their way out, he didn't know. Maybe they would wander around in there until they fell apart and rotted away to nothing. It sure looked as if some of them were on the way.

He put his eye back to the scope and panned to the left, toward the south end of town. That's when he saw it. Four SUVs were heading north on—he checked his map—Kolb, into town. They were passing the Air Force base. The vehicles went under a bridge and disappeared from view.

"Well, hello there," he said to the wind. "It looks like we've got a little company." It was impossible to see where the convoy was heading; the edge of the mountain range obstructed his view, but north was a safe bet. He pulled out his radio, a military-grade two-way, and cranked up the volume.

"Jimmy to base," he said, before adding, "over," like in the movies. There was no response for a moment, and then the radio squawked.

"Go ahead."

"Uh, yeah. I'm at my scouting post, and I just spotted a convoy heading north into the city. Four vehicles, unarmored, I think. I don't have an angle on where they're heading, but they look like locals." He didn't know why he said that. It just came out. It was something about their speed and the way they were traveling together. He waited.

"Got it. Good job."

"What next?"

"Finish your shift and then come on in. Call if you see anything else."

Jimmy was puzzled. Weren't they going to do anything? Was that it? Just note down what he had seen and go back to work? He paused, his finger hovering over the transmit button. After a long moment, he decided to let it go. Better not to ask questions.

"Understood," he answered. "I'll be back in a few hours."

"Ride safe."

That settled, Jimmy turned his attention back to the scope. Then he changed his mind. One more hit, to celebrate. He pulled out his kit and began to reload…

Twenty-Five

Hollister put down her report and ran her fingers through her greasy, disheveled hair.

"Fuck me," she muttered with a frown. She poured two fingers of tequila into a red plastic cup and swirled it around before downing it. Then she poured two more. *There's no way these numbers are right.* Three more people had vanished overnight. Counting the group she had executed on Friday, she was down twelve people for the week. She needed to grow her forces, and she needed to do it fast if she wanted to maintain her momentum. Unfortunately, she was going the wrong direction. *The ungrateful bastards.* The deserters pissed her off like nothing else. She took them in, fed them, and protected them, and all she asked in return was a little loyalty. Sure, life was tough right now. It was tough for everyone. But she didn't ask anyone to do anything she wouldn't do herself.

Except maybe cutting rings and jewelry off of the fingers of the dead. She smiled. That job she wouldn't touch with a ten-foot pole. Pollard had asked her once why she wanted the jewelry, useless as it was in today's world. The truth was, she didn't really know. She didn't have a good reason to collect it other than it made her feel good. For some reason, seeing the dead adorned in the accoutrements of their former life triggered an overwhelming sense of loss within her. The only way to make the feeling go away was to remove the jewelry, to take it from the dead and put it somewhere safe.

She supposed she was sick. No. More than 'supposed.' She knew she was sick, but who wasn't? And besides, she couldn't march down to the ship's counselor and schedule a therapy session, now could she? No. All she could do was run with it, see where it took her and trust it would turn out all right. There was a knock at her door.

"Enter!"

Pollard came in and stood at attention before her desk. He was a vague shadow of his former military self in stained jeans, a slightly less stained t-shirt, and scuffed brown cowboy boots. Thick leather gloves protruded from his pocket.

"What is it?" Hollister asked impatiently.

Pollard cleared his throat. He seemed to be having a hard time reverting to military formalities, as if it was some foreign concept rather than the lifestyle under which he had invested greater than half of his life. "I just got word from the radio room that one of our scouts spotted survivors in Tucson."

Hollister raised an eyebrow and sat up straighter. *This could be a solution to my personnel problem*, she thought. *Right out of the blue.* "Really? How many?"

"Four vehicles, heading north on the southeast side. They were traveling in formation, according to our scout."

"Interesting…" She stood and went to the far wall where a map of southern Arizona was plastered. Tiny blue pins covered areas she had cleared. Yellow pins indicated areas yet to be investigated, and red indicated sectors deemed too dangerous, areas overrun with undead or too radioactive. There were a lot of red pins on the map. Tucson however was represented by a single yellow pin. It was the great unknown. She couldn't have asked for better results.

"How did the city look?" In her mind's eye, she saw a burnt-out shell seething with undead. Although the bombs hadn't rained down in this part of the state, it seemed that human nature in the face of crisis was to destroy everything, like a small child who destroys his own toy rather than share it.

"Mostly intact, believe it or not," Pollard answered. "A fair amount of undead. Nothing we can't handle."

Hollister's mood brightened. Although they were in a highly defensible location in Sierra Vista, well off the major undead swarm paths, she was very interested in securing a supply route into the sprawling Tucson metro area. Very interested. Food, weapons, and supplies would be abundant in the former city of a million. Sierra Vista, while well-stocked, just didn't have the same depth to offer. Tucson also offered control over the main east-west transit route through this part of the country—Interstate 10. She turned to face Pollard.

"Well then, what are we waiting for?"

Pollard gave her a tight grin. "I'm already on it. We're pulling together an armed squad to go in and find out who these people are and where they're located."

Hollister thought about this for a moment. She held up a finger. "No. I've got a better idea."

Pollard's face clouded over, his idea scuttled before it left the ground.

"If they're mobile, then they probably have good resources, both people and materiel. I'd like to send in a mole, someone discreet who can figure out who's who and what their true strengths are, before we go up against them. A spy."

In truth, she was primarily interested in keeping her army intact, in not losing any more people, until she figured out a way to turn things around. She had to act fast to prevent the people in Tucson from learning about them, from presenting a more attractive destination for her people.

She chided herself. She didn't know anything about these others yet, and she was already making plans, getting ahead of herself. They could be stronger than her, though. She shuddered at the thought.

"We need to tread carefully here, Andrew. I want to take these people, whoever they are, but I want to do it with minimal casualties on our side."

Pollard nodded. "I like it." She could tell he was warming to the idea.

She gave him a final nudge. "You can do this, Andrew. I know it." He stood up straighter.

"Find someone you can trust. Give them a radio, and send them over. As soon as possible, tonight if you can."

Pollard chewed on his new orders for a moment before a big grin blossomed on his face. "I've got just the man."

"Keep me posted," Hollister said as she poured herself another shot of tequila.

"I will."

She held up a finger. "And one more thing."

"Yes?"

"What about that boy you were going to bring me? Woo?"

Pollard gestured at a chair. "Do you mind if I sit?"

Hollister was curious. "Feel free."

He settled into the chair facing her desk. "I think I have a better use for him..."

Twenty-Six

Late the next night

Jack hated I-10. Despised it. Like a straight shot through hell, it arrowed through the desert with barely a break. Traveling at night, he was making good time, though, far better than he had expected. Becka and Ellie were two days behind him now, buried in makeshift graves on the side of the freeway. He hoped he had gone deep enough to keep them away from the animals, but he wasn't sure. He tried not to think about it.

He was all alone now. Squeezing his eyes shut, he fought back the tears that had marked his existence since burying the last of his family. It worked this time, but just barely.

The truck he was driving, an ancient Ford F-250, hummed along the ruler-straight highway like a cruise missile. The undead hordes of Albuquerque were far behind now, and surprisingly, he had seen very few since getting on the Interstate. The lack of zombies bothered him, but he wasn't about to complain, not after Albuquerque. In places, he was forced to slow down to navigate around sand dunes that were growing across the roadway. The marks of man wouldn't last long without maintenance, he realized. Still, he was surprised with the speed at which it was degrading.

The truck downshifted as he began the climb into the Dragoon mountain range. Large boulders, some the size of houses, some larger, loomed on either the side of the road. Jack cringed at the idea of being trapped in the boulder field with a pack of the undead on his heels. It would be a nightmare of blind corners and innumerable death traps. A few minutes later, the motor stopped whining, and he began the descent. Tucson was only twenty miles ahead.

Thumbing the radio on, he pushed the scan button, and let the tuner cycle through the frequencies, searching for any hint of a signal. The digital display rolled through all available frequencies twice before he gave up and thumbed it off. He hadn't expected anything, but it was worth a try. *Tucson.* Jack hadn't been there in years, not since his early college days when he had dated a girl from the University of Arizona for a few months.

He had good memories of the place, having visited in February, when the weather was at its finest. He supposed it was nothing like that these days; it was probably overrun with the undead, trash everywhere, corpses lining the streets.

This close to town, the possibility of encountering a stray zombie on the road was much higher. As a precaution, he dropped his speed from fifty to forty and strained to look down the road ahead. On several occasions he thought he saw movement in the desert, dark wraiths gliding through the scrub, but he never stopped to investigate. The fuckers could wander around out here until they rotted away to dust as far as he was concerned.

Ten miles. Signs of civilization were becoming more frequent. He slowed again, dropping to thirty miles per hour. He scanned the road, expecting the worst at any moment. Nothing. Then, he saw something ahead that changed everything.

Lights. More than one. Moving. Bobbing. Heading west.

He gunned it.

Twenty-Seven

A pall of despair settled over the Scorpion Canyon community in the wake of Cesar's death. People who only days earlier had been ready and willing to take an active role in their survival were now backtracking, falling into old habits. There was even talk of leaving.

In hindsight, it all made perfect sense to Megan. Cesar had been the nexus of their community, the only one who fully understood their immediate needs while also looking days and weeks ahead to predict what was to come. Without him, they were adrift. She was lost. She had no idea how to pull things back together, to restore the nascent sense of hope crushed by his untimely death. And she didn't have any time left to figure it out.

"Goddamn you, Cesar!" she cursed. "Why'd you have to go and die on me? Why now?"

A single tear escaped her eye, racing down her cheek and plopping on the center of the pages of Cesar's notebook, which she had been reading. It clung there, glistening in the candle light, a shimmering convex lens magnifying his looping script. She had found the stack of notebooks beside his bed after leaving him in the desert. Inside were meticulous records and plans for the Scorpion Canyon community, ranging from supply inventories to hand-drawn maps of emergency escape routes through the Catalina Mountains and beyond. The notebooks were a treasure trove of unexpected information, and they made her miss Cesar all the more. Feeling frustrated and overwhelmed, she snapped the book shut and returned it to its place on top of the stack.

She got up, went to the door, unlocked it and pulled it open. A soft breeze pushed into the room, bringing with it the intoxicating aroma of creosote and sage. It had rained somewhere close by, she realized. She took a deep breath, drawing in the scent, savoring it. It allowed her to forget her troubles for just a moment. She loved so many things about the desert, but her favorite was the rain; the way the landscape sprang to life at the slightest hint of moisture, exploding into a kaleidoscope of exotic colors and smells, never ceased to amaze her.

A truck engine rumbled somewhere in the distance. It was drawing closer, the sound reverberating up the canyon. Megan tensed. The sun had gone down a half-hour ago. The noise would draw the undead like an army of ants to a pile of sugar. Headlights swept across the front of her building. The truck was just outside the main gate. She set off at a run, yelling at the top of her lungs for help.

The two men on guard duty were already hauling the rolling fence back by the time she arrived, making room for the rumbling vehicle to slip through.

"No! Wait!" she yelled.

The truck, an old blue Ford F-150 King-Cab, pulled into the compound, and the man at the wheel killed the engine.

"What the hell is going on out here?" Pringle asked. He ran up to the driver's door and banged on the window, making motions for the man inside to roll it down. A second later, the driver's door creaked open on dry hinges, and Megan saw two men inside, one older and one a teen. *Damn it! I don't need this now!*

"You fool!" Pringle shouted. "Do you realize you just rang the dinner bell for every zombie within a five-mile radius?"

Megan put a hand on his shoulder. "Calm down, Mike. They didn't know. We can deal with this."

Pringle shook her off. "No, Megan. We can't. These morons just killed us!"

"I've got it," Kevin announced from her rear.

They turned in unison. "What do you mean?"

"I mean, don't worry about it. I'll go out and draw them away, and then I'll loop back around once it's quiet."

Megan and Pringle exchanged a look of uncertainty. The damage was already done; that couldn't hurt. "Do it," she ordered.

She turned to the driver. "Mike is right. You've put us all at risk."

The man opened his mouth to protest, but seemed to think better of it. "I'm sorry," he said. "I wasn't thinking. Can I do anything to help?"

Pringle shook his head in disgust. "No. You've done enough already."

The driver was a big man, standing a little over six-feet-tall, with collar-length brown hair and a simple, open face. The other man was younger, much younger and Asian. He looked to be in his late teens or early twenties. He was slender, almost effeminate, yet something in his eyes disturbed her, put her on guard.

"Jack Wolfe," the driver said, holding out his hand.

Megan shook it. "I'm Megan Pritchard. This is Mike Pringle." She waved at the other people who had come outside to investigate. "And this is our camp."

"This is Peter Woo," Jack said, tossing his head at the young man in the passenger seat. "I picked him up on I-10 a few miles east of town." Peter inclined his head and smiled, but didn't say anything. Again, that bad feeling.

Kevin roared up on his motorcycle, stopping at the closed gate. The guards hustled over and hauled it open, and a moment later he vanished into the night.

Jack locked eyes with Megan. "Thanks." He sighed. "I've been on the road for a long time…" Megan softened. These men were the first new arrivals in over two weeks. Showing anger was the wrong way to welcome them, even if they did almost bring a swarm with them.

A gun fired far in the distance, the *pop pop pop* the loudest sound for miles. Megan sucked in a breath. A few seconds later, a shrill horn blared loud and long, cutting through the night like a knife. Kevin. His engine noise wound up like an angry hornet, and then just as quickly faded away into the night as he led the zombies away.

Megan released the breath she had been holding. "I hope he's okay…"

"Let's get this truck out of the way," Pringle said, shattering the moment. He gestured at Woo. "Get behind the wheel, kid. Put it in neutral." Woo complied.

"You ready?" Pringle asked. He pointed to a spot on the east side of the ranger station. "We're gonna push it over there, and we're going to do it as quietly as possible."

Jack shrugged. "Yeah. Sure."

"I'll help," Megan said, slipping between the men at the tailgate. She sensed an unexpected hostility between them, and she wanted to get a handle on it before it manifested as something more overt. Once they got the truck in place, Woo climbed out. He was taller than Megan expected, almost as tall as Jack.

She turned to Pringle. "Where do you want to put them tonight?"

Pringle scratched his chin while he considered his response. "How about the main lobby? There's room in the book section…"

"Is that okay with you guys?" Megan asked.

They looked at each other. Jack answered, "We'll sleep wherever you put us."

"Yeah," Woo added.

Megan started tugging at the rope securing the tarp. "Okay, then...let's get your stuff unloaded, and you can tell us your story—or not, if you'd rather rest up first."

Jack yawned and looked at Woo. "If you don't mind, I'd rather get some sleep. It's been a rough couple of days..."

"Sure. That works."

With that settled, they set to work unloading the truck.

Twenty-Eight

The next day

How did I not see this coming? Megan chided herself, exasperated. *How did I let things go this far?* "Listen, Mike. This is what Cesar wanted," she said in a controlled tone.

Directly across from her, Pringle shot her one of his award-winning smiles, the one that said, "You're wrong and I'm right, and you just don't know it yet." She hated that look. *Hated* it.

"I beg to differ. That's what Cesar wanted when he was about to die. But he's gone, and I believe that as the community grows, we need a different style of leadership, something new, something… stronger."

Megan seethed inside. *Prick.* "Look, Mike. This isn't the military. It's just not. That's not what we—"

He interrupted, "Bullshit!" His voice dropped an octave. "You and I both know this isn't working. The people are looking for a strong leader, and you're not cutting it. Ask anyone."

Megan railed internally at the accusation, partly because it pissed her off, but more importantly, because there was a grain of truth to it. Neither she, nor Cesar before her, ruled with an iron fist. It hadn't been Cesar's style, and it certainly wasn't hers, not in a million years.

Mike shook his fist. "Pay attention, Megan. This is important. People are talking. They want change, and they want it now." Megan's mind was spinning. She hadn't heard any rumors of discontent with her leadership, at least none spoken to her face. *Maybe that's the problem? Maybe people are afraid to come to me?*

There were certainly people who didn't fit in. Misfits, people who she never would have socialized with before the apocalypse. But still, even they deserved a chance at safety, at survival. Everyone did. She swallowed her anger, running her palms across her lap in an effort to calm herself. "Let's just assume, for a second, that there's something to what you're saying…"

Pringle leaned forward. Across the room, Alicia studiously flipped through a dog-eared issue of *People* magazine.

"If that were the case," Megan continued, "I would have heard something. I'm out in the community every day, working the fences, collecting food, bringing in new people. Why hasn't anyone come to me? Tell me that." She cursed herself for sinking to Pringle's level, but she had crossed the point of no return.

"You just can't—"

There was a sharp crack from outside. Then another, followed by a sustained burst of AK-47 fire.

"Shit! What now?" Megan yelped, leaping from her chair. "We'll finish this later!" She drew her gun and raced for the front door. Pringle was right behind her. The gunfire had stopped by the time they reached the door, as if it had never happened. Megan peered out the window on the left side while Pringle looked out the right.

"I don't see anything," he said.

"Me either."

"On three." Pringle stepped back from the door and dropped into a firing position, covering the portal as Megan flung it open. Nothing. Pringle scuttled forward and scanned the porch beyond. "Clear!" he announced.

They leapfrogged into the street, covering each other, searching for the source of the exchange. It was down the street. Jack, the new man, squatted on his haunches beside two corpses, inspecting them. A few feet beyond, a young man, another recent arrival whose name Megan couldn't recall, sat in the road, cradling his arm. *What the hell?* Jack got to his feet as they arrived on the scene, a sad, disgusted look on his face.

"What happened?" Pringle demanded, addressing the man on the ground and ignoring Jack.

"I—" the man started.

Jack stepped between them and straightened to his full height, towering over Pringle. "It was an accident. There was no one at the gate."

He was talking about the east gate, a large iron security door liberated from a border patrol storage depot and installed on the perimeter fence.

"Are you bitten?" Megan asked the man, already knowing the answer. She had to hear the words from his mouth. Tears came to the man's eyes, and he choked up, but nodded. Megan dropped her head to her chest and stared at the ground, seeing nothing and everything at the same time.

This was the first infection inside the compound in over a month, the first breach under her watch, and not only did it mean the man was as good as dead, but it also gave Pringle ammunition in his argument against her leadership.

"The gate is secure now," Jack interjected. "But there's no sign of the sentry." It was standard practice to post a rotating sentry on the gate at all times. *Everyone* in the community took a turn.

"Who was on today?" Megan asked. She felt as if she was watching someone else ask the question, floating above, observing a nasty tragedy unfold beneath her.

Pringle thought for a second before answering. Gate security was his domain. "Tony." Tony had been with the community for about five weeks. A man of few words, Megan didn't know much about him, but he had always been reliable. "Has anyone seen him today?" she asked.

They all shook their heads. *Great.* She couldn't help feel that this whole thing was rigged. The timing was too much of a coincidence. "Okay," she said. "We contained it this time." She met Jack's eyes and held them. "Thanks for your quick action."

He shrugged and holstered his weapon. His eyes revealed nothing, a pair of one-way mirrors on his soul. "What happens to him?" Jack asked quietly, eyes flitting to the sobbing man.

"He's infected. There's nothing we can—"

Before she could finish her sentence, Pringle drew his weapon, stepped up to the man, and pulled the trigger. The report echoed through the compound and up the canyon beyond.

Megan screamed. "What the hell was that?"

Pringle holstered his gun and turned to her. "No more fucking around, Megan. It's time to get serious about this community, and it starts right here, right now."

Megan didn't know how to respond to this challenge. Pringle's unilateral action amounted to an execution of an innocent man. Sure, the man had been infected and was as good as dead anyway, but the community had rules. Infected who were mobile had the choice between taking their own lives or having someone else do it for them. Pringle, in his haste, had stripped him of his rights, stolen the last vestiges of the man's humanity, for his own gain.

"That's not how we do things here!"

Pringle stared back at her. "It is now!"

Jack took a step back, out of their direct path. It was all Megan could do not to draw her weapon and shoot Pringle. Right here. Right now. But she knew it would do no good. She would lose the trust of the community, would become, in their eyes, no better than him.

"Guys." It was Jack. Megan turned to him, her gaze full of fire.

She exploded. "What?"

He stepped forward, putting himself between them, and raised his hands in a sign of peace.

That set Pringle off. "Who the fuck do you think you are?" He took a step forward and shoved Jack in the chest.

Yeah, Megan thought. *Who the fuck?* But inside, she was glad for the interruption. It gave her a precious few seconds, seconds she desperately needed, to cool off before she did something rash.

"You're right," Jack said, addressing Pringle. "I'm nobody, just a guy who has a feeling that you guys are about to do something you'll regret." He motioned around them with a slight toss of his head. "In case you haven't noticed, you've got an audience." It was true. A circle had formed around them; the other members of the community were watching with bated breath.

Megan took a deep breath and steadied herself. "You're right. Let's take this inside."

Pringle glanced around and deflated as he realized the stakes. He shook his head. "Not now. I've got to get someone on the gate. We'll talk later." He glared, his eyes full of murder, then shifted his gaze to Jack. He abruptly spun on his heels and stalked off toward the fence.

"Thanks," Megan mouthed to Jack, as Pringle moved out of earshot. "That was close."

Jack held her gaze for a moment, and then moved toward the dead man. "Let's get these bodies out of here."

Twenty-Nine

Later That Night

Cast by the intense moonlight filtering through the security bars covering his window, vertical bars of shadow lined the far wall of Pringle's room. He was in a prison of his own making, he realized. He was one of the few brave enough to sleep in a room with a window on the outside perimeter. The truth was, without a view to the outdoors, even with the ever-present threat of the undead, he would go crazy. Cursing, he rolled over and scrunched up his pillow as he desperately tried to find a more comfortable position. He had to get some sleep.

"Fucking bitch," he cursed for the thousandth time. "Why can't she see that she just doesn't have what it takes to run a community this size? Is she blind? That breach today should be all she needs." He slammed his fist down on the bed.

The breech. He couldn't have planned it better if he had tried. Unfortunately, he had had no hand in the event. It was just one of those things. Still, it had worked out well for him...sort of.

Putting a bullet through the infected man's head, well, that had been a stroke of pure genius. He had always felt that letting the infected choose their own death was ridiculous, a stupid bow to a civilization that no longer existed. *You get bit, it's over.* He just hoped someone would have the balls to do the same for him if he was ever in that situation. Coming back as one of the undead was the worst fate he could imagine.

That won't be a problem, he decided with a devious smile. *There's a whole camp full of people itching to put a bullet in my head now.* The thought calmed him. This new world needed people like him, even if they didn't know it yet. Someone had to make the hard decisions, and they had to make them without hesitation. Or they would all die.

There was another reason for Pringle's anger, one he loathed to admit—Megan's repeated rejection in the face of his most charming advances. It was obvious, he thought, that they should be together, yet no matter what he did, or how much he turned on the charm, she wouldn't give him the time of the day. And now... now, this new guy Jack showed up. It was obvious Megan had something for him. The way she looked at him... the way her eyes lingered on his. Any moron could see she wanted to fuck him.

Every time he saw them together, he wanted to reach out and grab her by the shoulders, shake her and scream, "Can't you see? I'm right here in front of you!" But it was no use. She would have none of it.

With an angry sigh, Pringle gave up on sleep and pulled a ragged copy of Sun Tzu's *The Art of War* and a flashlight from beside his bed, thumbed to the dog-eared page in the middle, and resumed reading. Never a big reader before the uprising, Pringle had been surprised to discover he had a voracious appetite for the written word. He was in the middle of four separate books at the moment, a combination of management and military strategy as well as law enforcement guides, all acquired during supply raids. It was the words in those books that had finally convinced him to make his play on Megan, along with a deep-rooted sense that he could do it better if given an opportunity. The books would fill that gap, he figured, provide the details on how to achieve his goal.

The simplest solution was to kill her, just make her go away once and for all. The problem was, so far, he had been unable to figure out how. He had come close after the breech, and if it weren't for that bastard Jack, he would have finished her off in the courtyard, taken control, and turned things around in a hurry. In hindsight, he was glad that hadn't happened. If there was one thing he had learned from Sun Tzu, it was the value of patience. He was close. It was only a matter of time.

The main problem was perception. If he killed Megan and was discovered, he would be cast from the community at best, and at worst, killed on the spot. Despite his reservations about her leadership abilities, she had a loyal following, people who would die for her. That, he could not afford to ignore. He sighed and tried to focus on his book.

As he turned the page, there was a knock at his door. Cocking his head, he listened to see if it was repeated. It came again. *Who?* He had a vision of Megan coming to his room in the middle of the night to relinquish her power. He dismissed it. *Unrealistic.* There was another knock, more insistent. It wasn't a woman's knock.

"Hold on, hold on," he said as he crossed the room. "Who's there?"

"Woo," came the answer.

Pringle opened the door a few inches and peered through. "What do you want? It's late."

Woo looked up and down the hall, as if he expected someone to come along at any moment. "Can I come in? It's important."

What the hell? He couldn't sleep. He figured he might as well see what the kid wanted. He opened the door wide, and Woo entered, glancing over his shoulder one last time.

Pringle motioned him to a chair on the far side of the room. "Drink? I've got tequila and water."

Woo considered the offer. "Tequila." From a half-empty bottle of Patrón, Pringle poured out two healthy shots and handed one to Woo. Drinking with the kid certainly wasn't what he had planned for the evening, but why not? He had nothing better to do until morning. And maybe the tequila would help him sleep. He had a fleeting thought, *What if the kid is coming on to me?* He took a step back, putting some distance between himself and the young man.

Woo sensed his discomfort and laughed. "Shit. Sorry. Don't worry. I'm not here for that. Not at all," he said, shaking his head emphatically.

"Then why are you here?" Pringle's curiosity was piqued. "It's late."

"I saw you and that woman Megan arguing earlier."

Pringle let out a sharp laugh. "Yeah? So did a lot of people. It happens."

Woo smiled. "I think I may have an answer to your problem."

Pringle downed his tequila in one gulp and refilled. "I'm listening."

A conspiratorial smile blossomed on Woo's lips. "I need your assurance—"

Pringle cut him off with a chop of his hand. "No assurances. Tell me what you came to say or get out."

Woo looked back at the door, as if reconsidering his decision. Then he turned back to Pringle and started talking. The next half hour flew by as Woo gave him the details on Hollister's group, painting a picture that filled in all of the holes Pringle saw in his current life, from the no-bullshit approach to community relations to her plans for expansion across the Southwest. Pringle peppered him with questions throughout, growing increasingly excited as Woo had answers for everything. *Either this kid is a master bullshit artist, or these guys have already figured things out.* Finally, he ran out of questions. He poured them each another shot of tequila, and then reclined in his chair, drumming his fingers on the arm.

Woo had revolutionized his understanding of the new world, provided the answers to his most vexing questions, and most importantly, given him hope, a new lease on life. His head reeled from the potential. Just forty miles away was a group of people who shared his approach to the world. He struggled to maintain a poker face, to keep his excitement from the teen.

"So what do you need from me?" he asked cautiously.

Woo grinned. "I'm glad you asked..."

Pringle leaned forward, unable to contain his excitement anymore as Woo laid out a plan so simple, so devious, he wondered why he hadn't thought of it himself.

Thirty

Megan awoke slowly, her semiconscious already sifting through the events of the previous day. The conflict with Pringle weighed heavily on her. She knew she would have to do something soon, make some movement toward a compromise; otherwise, they were all doomed.

Her thoughts turned to Jack. He intrigued her. She replayed their exchange after the zombie incursion. It had triggered something lurking deep within. It made no sense, yet somehow his presence felt *right* at a primal level, his quiet strength, the way he held his ground against Pringle's challenge, the casual manner in which he met her gaze, his eyes filled with a lingering sadness. She wanted to be close to him. No. She *needed* to be close to him. To *be* with him.

Her face grew hot; she blushed. A devious smile blossomed on her lips. Almost without thinking, she slipped a hand beneath the covers, tracing her fingers along the plane of her belly, then pressing them to the warmth building between her legs. She closed her eyes, imagining Jack above her. For the briefest instant, some small part of her attempted to dismiss the fantasy, to relegate it to a simple infatuation. But it was no use. Her desire triumphed, and she abandoned all pretense at control, succumbing to the rush of the moment. She began to touch herself, slowly at first, then increasing the tempo. Her breath came in ragged gasps. Sweat broke out on her forehead. Her vision dimmed, pinpricks of light flashed at the edges, and then it snapped back into stark clarity as she reached climax. A small moan escaped her lips. She shuddered. "Jack..."

Megan lay still for what seemed an eternity. She panted softly, basking in the afterglow with her eyes closed and a contented smile lingering on her lips. As her euphoria began to fade, she found herself wondering 'what if'? *What if Jack feels the same way? How would it work? Could it work?* She opened her eyes, her smile crumbling. It's *impossible.* Or is it? She chewed her lip, considering her predicament. Everything was different now. We've all done things we never would have done before. *All of us. Some worse than others.* Regardless, she could easily imagine the look of disgust on his face when she told him of her past. *Revulsion. Condemnation.*

She shook her head and tried to dismiss the image. *There's nothing I can do about that now. It's part of who I am. Who I was.*

With a dismayed groan, Megan kicked the sheets from her feet and sat up. She shivered, chilled as the light sheen of sweat evaporated. *I'll deal with this later,* she told herself as she got up. *Right now I have work to do.*

Today's job was a supply run into the center of town. They were planning to loot a construction tool rental company in hopes of finding a trailer-mounted diesel generator. Up until now, the community had survived without electricity, taking water from the stream in the canyon and using candles for light. A generator would give them flexibility to draw from the well as well as the ability to use power tools and the equipment necessary to maintain the vehicles. She even held out hope that they could power up the bank of dark computers in the back of the ranger station and use the satellite dish on the roof to connect to the internet, if it still existed. It would be nice to see if there was anything left of the outside world.

With a renewed sense of purpose, Megan sprang from her bed and began to dress—thick, canvas cargo pants and a cotton tank top. She laced up a pair of heavy hiking boots as well to protect against broken glass. After a quick scan of the room, she decided she was ready to go.

Despite the new complications in her life, Megan found herself whistling as she strapped on her guns and hefted her armored jacket from the chair beside the bed. *This is going to get interesting.*

Thirty-One

Keep your friends close and your enemies even closer…

Megan repeated this mantra to herself as she drove the old white Park Service truck through the ruins of downtown Tucson. She had been tempted to remain in camp and send Pringle off by himself, but at the last minute she had decided it was best to come along, to attempt some sort of reconciliation through shared sacrifice. It had sounded good back at camp. Now she wasn't so sure.

In addition to herself and Pringle, Kevin was on his motorcycle serving as a forward scout. He stayed a block ahead of them the entire time, searching for traffic blockages, clusters of undead, anything that could slow them down. Twice so far, he had come roaring back to the convoy, adjusted their course, and sent them down a different combination of streets to avoid an unseen threat.

Megan rode with Pringle, an icy silence wedged between them the entire way. Jack drove the second truck with Beth Fontaine and her boyfriend Marty Jackson, both out of Wilcox. The rental center parking lot was empty, a locked gate serving to keep it free of the undead. Kevin popped the lock in no time, waved them in, and pulled the gate shut behind them. They waited in silence for three full minutes, the clock on the dash ticking as they prepared for the incursion.

The plan was simple. Megan, along with Kevin and Pringle, would go in and clear the building while the others remained on lookout. At the front doors, Megan reviewed the plan one more time. One by one, she stared each person in the eye, reaffirming their interdependence. It was an old trick she had learned right after the 9/11 attacks. She and her sister had been on the way to a vacation in Cancun with their parents. Soon after the cabin doors closed, the pilot had appeared at the front of the cabin. For ten minutes, he walked through the aircraft making eye contact with each and every passenger, reassuring them that he was in control, that they had nothing to worry about. Both she and her sister had been terrified to fly at the time, but the pilot's actions had put her at ease, allowed her to relax and even enjoy her flight.

She saved Jack for last. It took everything she had not to smile like a stupid kid when she met his eyes. Her face burned. She made it quick, and then turned away.

The front door was already unlocked. They stepped inside. The store appeared untouched, as if the owners had stepped out for lunch only minutes before. The air smelled of grease and gasoline. Lawnmowers, dirt, and something else, an undercurrent, sickly-sweet, slightly cloying, with hints of cinnamon and dried beef. A zombie.

Kevin reached into his pocket and pulled out a handful of ball bearings. With a quick glance at Megan and Pringle, he tossed them deep into the shop, up and over the tall, steel equipment racks. The steel balls shattered the silence of the store as they ricocheted off counters and shelves at the rear. The zombie moaned.

"Damn it," Kevin muttered. "I hate the ones that have been closed up. They smell the worst."

Megan grimaced. She hated the indoor ones as well. For some reason, they seemed *moister,* fleshy bags of putrefying rot that tended to explode into chunks of slimy, decaying flesh at the slightest impact, a far cry from their outdoor brethren who toughened up like an old leather belt under the desert sun.

"Here we go," she said.

They fanned out. Megan stayed in the center while Pringle went right and Kevin headed left.

"It sounds like only one," Kevin whispered. Footsteps. Coming closer. The creature moaned again. It was straight ahead. Megan choked down on the grip of her three-pound splitting maul, readying her muscles for action. She glanced to the right, looking for Pringle. He was gone.

What the fuck? "Where's Pringle?" she hissed at Kevin. Before he could answer, the creature stumbled from the gloom. Morbidly obese in its former life, and standing somewhere north of six-and-a-half-feet tall, it shuffled toward her, ignoring Kevin entirely. The name on the patch over the creature's breast pocket was "Rod."

As it came within range, Megan put her weight on her back foot and swung down with her maul, letting loose a blood-curdling scream of rage and frustration in the process. Her swing hit home, plunging into the side of the creature's head, splitting it open like a melon.

She took a step back and yanked her tool from the creature's head with a wet sucking sound, wrenching with all of her might. The zombie kept coming. For a terrifying moment, she thought she had missed, that the creature was still attacking, and then, like a tree blowing over in the wind, it pitched forward and crashed to the ground where she had just been standing.

"Nice!" Kevin exclaimed.

Megan allowed herself a brief smile, and turned to scan the front of the store again. "Now where the hell did Mike go?"

Kevin shrugged. "Shit, I don't know. I wasn't paying attention." He took a step into the rear of the store, disappearing into the shadows.

"Light," Megan reminded him.

"Oh, yeah." He unclipped an LED Maglite from his belt and flicked it on. She did the same. They played their beams along the aisles leading to the rear where the generators would be stored. There was no sign of Pringle.

"Mike," she called out softly, then again more forcefully. "This isn't funny." Pringle was known for his practical jokes, although why he would pick this moment to play one was beyond her. She stalked over to the front door and opened it. "Did Mike come out here?"

"No," Jack answered with a concerned frown. "He's not with you?"

She shook her head. "No. He disappeared."

"Do you want me to come in? Look for him?"

Megan looked over his shoulder at the street beyond, weighing the risks. She wanted at least three people outside, just in case. "No. Better you stay here." Jack didn't look convinced, but he agreed.

"Back in a minute," Megan said, letting the door swing closed.

Wait... Where's Kevin?

She took a step toward the rear. "Kevin?" There was a muffled coughing from somewhere in the back. "Kevin?" she cried again, getting worried. "Is that you?"

She stood stock still for a few moments, trying to decipher the sound. It wasn't a zombie. They didn't make that noise. No. It sounded like someone had sucked a drink down the wrong pipe and was trying to clear their throat. *Like they were choking.*

She took off at a run, straight down the center aisle. It was a bad idea, she knew, but she had no choice. As she reached the rental counter stretching across the rear of the building, she saw movement out of the corner of her eye, a door swinging shut. *The storage room.*

"Mike?" she called out in barely a whisper. "Kevin?" She was answered by a deathly silence. Megan took a deep breath, steeled her nerves, and stepped to the door. She listened carefully. There was someone, or *something*, inside moving around, faintly scratching. Shuffling. *Another zombie?* She drew her pistol and thumbed off the safety. She wished she hadn't told Jack to wait outside; she considered, just for a moment, turning around and getting him. *There's no time. Mike and Kevin may be in trouble...* As quietly as possible, she pushed on the door, cringing as the hinges squealed.

The room beyond was as dark as a moonless night. She played her flashlight across the far wall. A figure, coming fast from her right. *Too fast to be a zombie.*

"What—" Before she could finish, her assailant crashed headlong into her, sending her tumbling to the floor in an ungraceful heap. Her gun discharged with a blinding flash, and her flashlight flew from her hands to clatter away into the darkness, throwing crazy patterns on the walls as it spun. *Crack!* A powerful blow connected with her jaw, snapping her mouth closed, driving her teeth through the tip of her tongue. Blood exploded into her mouth.

In the time it took her to realize what was going on, her attacker snatched her pistol from her hand and tossed it away on the cool concrete. He straddled her and pinned her hands behind her head, digging a knee in to her stomach to keep her pinned to the floor. Megan squirmed and bucked, trying to break free, and was rewarded with another vicious blow to the face.

"I've got her!" her attacker yelled. It was a young man's voice, one she knew. There was a soft click, and the overhead lights blazed to life, flooding the room with harsh white light.

Megan blinked and gasped in shock. It was Peter Woo, the new kid. "Peter?"

Woo grinned at her and held a finger up to his lips.

"Megan." The voice came from behind her.

Megan craned her neck. "Mike?" Pringle stepped into her field of view slowly, as if he had all the time in the world.

She spit a glob of blood on the floor. "What the hell are you doing? Where's Kevin?"

"I said quiet!" Woo said, digging his knee in deeper. Megan grunted at the pain, but didn't take her eyes from Pringle. Squatting down beside her, Pringle brushed a strand of hair from her eyes. Alternating waves of sorrow and triumph radiated from his face.

He shook his head sadly. “I told you things had to change, but you just wouldn’t listen…”

Thirty-Two

Jack dug around in his back pocket and fished out a tin of chewing tobacco. He ran his fingernail around the lid, slicing the paper seal. Marty watched him intently.

"Dip?" Jack offered, holding out the open can.

Marty shot a furtive glance in Beth's direction, and then shook his head. "Thanks. No."

Jack extended his offer to Beth as well. She declined with a wry grin. He took a pinch and packed it into his lower lip, spitting out the stray flakes. A gun boomed from somewhere deep inside.

"What the hell was that?" Marty asked. He took a step toward the door and plastered his face against the window, cupping it with his hands to eliminate the glare. "Guys! Look!"

Jack opened the door and stuck his head inside. There was no sign of the others. He held a finger to his lips. "Shhhh."

A second later he yanked the door the rest of the way open. "Something's wrong. I'm going in," he said. "Keep an eye on the lot." Marty grunted his acknowledgment.

The first thing Jack saw was the zombie corpse sprawled on the floor. He noted that it was a clean kill, the head caved in from a frontal assault, gelatinous chunks of brain oozing from a large fissure in the crown. He cocked his head, absorbing the sounds, the feel of the empty store. The gunshot meant something had gone terribly wrong. This was supposed to be a stealth raid.

He heard something. A rhythmic thudding echoed from somewhere in the rear, like someone repeatedly dropping a bag of sand on the ground. "Megan?" he called out. "Pringle?"

The thudding stopped. A second later, it started up again.

"What the..?" Jack took off at a run, choosing the aisle on the far right, directly underneath a line of dust- and grease-caked windows. As he rounded the corner at the rental counter, his legs suddenly flew out from underneath him, sending him sliding into a spinning wire rack of work gloves and safety goggles, knocking it to the floor with an earsplitting crash. He landed hard on the polished concrete, his head bouncing with a resounding crack. His flashlight blinked out on impact. He scrambled to get up, but couldn't get his feet under him. He kept slipping on something.

Blood. Fighting the urge to vomit, Jack shook his flashlight to restore it. Light flooded out, and he saw the source of the blood. It was Kevin. He was on his back, tucked against the base of a shelf, his throat sliced from ear to ear, the last of his blood draining slowly across the floor.

Zombies don't use knives. Jack got to his feet and touched his head, feeling for blood. Finding none of his own, he forged ahead. Kevin's dead. No use stopping. Megan and Mike might still be alive. As he pushed through the storeroom door, the source of the thumping noise became brutally obvious.

Pringle hovered over Megan's inert form raining blows down on her face. Peter Woo stood behind him, observing the beating with rapt attention.

Jack leveled his gun at Pringle and yelled, "Stop!" Pringle halted mid-punch and looked at Jack with wild eyes. A manic smile danced at the edges of his mouth. Woo slowly reached for his weapon, but withdrew his hand when Jack cocked the hammer on his pistol. Woo took a step back toward the door leading to the outside of the building.

Without changing his aim, Jack flicked his gaze to Megan. He bit back a surge of queasiness as he took in her face. One eye was swollen shut, buried beneath a bruise that seemed to grow as he watched. Blood coated her face from two split lips, and a ragged gash ran from her temple all the way to her left jaw. He could only imagine her agony.

He shifted his gaze to her chest to determine if she was still breathing. He counted. One...two... three. Finally, her chest rose. Jack let out a sigh of relief.

"What the hell are you doing?" he shouted at Pringle.

Pringle laughed a high-pitched, rabid cackle. "It's none of your damned business. Now get back out front and do your job!" Megan coughed and spit up a geyser of bright red blood.

Jack tightened his grip on his pistol. "Get away from her. Now!"

Out of the corner of his eye, he saw the handle on the steel door at the rear of the storeroom twist violently just before the door flew open, crashing against the wall with an earsplitting clang.

In the time it took Jack to process what was happening, three ghouls spilled into the room and descended upon Woo, who stood nearest to the door. They drug him to the ground and tore into his flesh with an insatiable ferocity. Woo screamed twice, and then went silent.

Two more undead slipped through, bringing the total to five. Pringle scrambled from the zombies, leaving Megan completely exposed.

Jack fired four times, dropping two of the zombies munching on Woo and hitting, but not destroying, the third. Pringle fired at the larger of the zombies at the door, dropping it with his first shot. His second shot went wild, ricocheting from the steel door in a brilliant cascade of sparks. And then his gun jammed.

"Shit!" he threw it aside and reached to his thigh, probably searching for the backup Jack knew he kept strapped there. Before Pringle could get off another shot, the third zombie near Woo rushed him and locked its teeth onto his forearm, ripping and tearing at the exposed flesh.

Pringle screamed and spun away, trying desperately to shake the creature loose. Jack took careful aim and put a bullet into the head of the remaining zombie by the door. Chunks of diseased brains splattered across a crate of small engine oil.

A cacophony of moans built outside the door, more zombies, drawn by the gunfire. Jack sprinted across the room and slammed the door shut just as another monster was about to step through. He flipped the deadbolt. Woo began to reanimate, and Jack shot him in the face before he could complete the process.

At that moment, Pringle managed to get his pistol up and under the jaw of the monster on his arm. He pulled the trigger twice, and the creature's head exploded in a fine mist, glazing his face in a slimy coating of gore.

"Goddamn it!" Pringle waved around his mangled arm. "Look what that son of a bitch did to me!" Wary of Pringle's next move, Jack nodded slowly. Regardless of Pringle's intentions against Megan, he was a doomed man now, and Jack could see by the dull gleam in his eye that Pringle understood this as well. Pringle spit out a chunk of bone shrapnel and scrubbed the gore from his face.

Megan groaned, the sound answered by the incessant moans of the horde of zombies just outside.

"I don't feel so good," Pringle said woozily.

Jack wasn't surprised. The zombie had plenty of time attached to his arm, and all of the motion would have served to accelerate the transfer of the infection from his blood to his brain. Pringle dropped into a cracked plastic chair at the far wall. His gun sat on his lap, his finger still hooked in the trigger guard. He snorted. Keeping one eye on Pringle, Jack took a tentative step toward Megan. As he reached her, he realized Pringle was crying.

He knelt down and whispered into her ear, "Hold tight...we're getting out of here." She groaned and tried to roll over. Pringle kept crying.

He scooped her from the floor and backed towards the door, taking care not to jostle her.

As he was about to leave, Pringle called out to him, "Jack."

Jack eyed him suspiciously. "Yeah?"

"I—tell her I'm sorry…It wasn't worth it…"

Jack looked down at Megan. Her eyes remained closed. She gave no indication she was aware of the events swirling around her.

"I will," Jack said with a tight frown. "I will."

Pringle pressed his gun to the soft flesh under his jaw, closed his eyes, and squeezed the trigger. The gun boomed, and the contents of his skull sprayed the wall behind him. His corpse tumbled from the chair, landing beside Woo in an undignified heap. Jack lingered at the door for a moment, surveying the carnage. Satisfied everything was over, he turned and made his way to the front of the store.

Marty and Beth were sharing a cigarette when he burst through the door. The parking lot was empty. The cigarette fell to the ground, discarded when they saw him and Megan.

"Oh, my God!" Beth gasped. "What happened? Where are the others?"

"They're dead. We need to go right now!"

"I'll get the truck," Marty said, racing off.

"I don't understand..." Beth trailed off. She came over to Jack and began inspecting Megan's wounds.

Marty pulled up and hopped out, leaving the truck running. He dashed around to the tailgate and unlatched it with a loud clang. "Put her in here. Beth was an EMT." Jack nodded and placed Megan gently in the truck bed. Beth followed. With a last concerned glance, Marty returned to the cab. Beth whacked the side of the bed twice, and they took off with a roar.

Thirty-Three

Sierra Vista

"This is bullshit!" Pollard said, slamming his fist on his desk.

The man seated across from him jumped in surprise. "Sir?"

Pollard stood and pointed at the door. "I've heard enough. Get out!"

His anger was fueled by the report he had just received. Food was running low, and despite his continued prodding, Hollister was ignoring him, instead focusing their collection efforts on drugs and weapons.

"We need these drugs," she had insisted during their last confrontation. "The people expect them. They need them..."

Pollard had exploded at this faulty logic, responding that an army traveled on its stomach, not its nose, something Hollister, with all of her graduate degrees and military experience should have known. The thing that burned him up most of all was she just didn't seem to care anymore. It was as if she had given up, consigned him and all of the other people following her to a slow and painful death. She seemed perfectly happy to fuck her way through the population, to inhale every gram of cocaine that passed her way, and to let this last vestige of civilization crumble into nothingness.

Pollard's anger mounted. Sending Woo to Tucson had been a mistake, he now realized. He should have used someone else. He hadn't heard from the teen since he had left. He had to assume the worst. For all he knew, the kid was a zombie now, stumbling around the desert, searching for his next meal.

In a blind rage, Pollard stormed from his office and stalked across the street, heading straight for Hollister's quarters. He pushed past her guard and burst into the front room without knocking. "Hollister!" he yelled. "Where are you?"

Music pulsed from the back room and the dank, earthy smell of marijuana permeated the air. Pollard's blood pressure spiked and a sense of righteous indignation washed through him. His vision constricted to a red-tinged tunnel. Boom, boom, boom. His heart hammered in his chest.

Outside of Hollister's bedroom door, he discovered a skeletal, barely-dressed young woman passed out on a cracked-leather loveseat. The woman's shirt rode up her midriff, exposing the bottom half of one plump, silicone-enhanced breast. A bottle of tequila was wedged in her crotch. Her weapon, a silver Colt 1911, lay on the floor, well out of her reach. Pollard trembled, his rage vibrating like a mad tuning fork. This has to stop!

He slammed into the door with his shoulder, and it exploded inward with a bang. He stepped inside Hollister's lair and sucked in his breath as he took the sight of a mass of bodies writhing on the bed. Snoop Dogg rapped from a battery-powered radio in the corner. Where the fuck does she find these people? He stood there for a moment, absorbing the scene, consumed by the rage burning through his body. He was past the point of no return.

A wall mirror covered by a massive mound of cocaine rested on a chair beside the bed. Sliced-open kilo bags lay discarded on the floor like clear snakeskins. Trash bags full of marijuana were stacked against the far wall. A thick layer of cloying smoke extended from the ceiling almost to the floor, making him gag. No one paid him any attention. Lost in the midst of their drug-fueled orgy, the people on the bed were oblivious to the armed man about to lose his temper for the last time.

Pollard heard a stirring behind him. It was the woman on the couch. She rolled over, let out a long brassy fart, and then fell back into her slumber. He fired five times, one shot for the woman in the hall and four more for the people on the bed. Each shot was like a miniature sun, illuminating the room in a red and orange flare of fury until the gloom snuffed it out. When it was all over, the smell of cordite permeated his nostrils, mercifully blotting out the dried-shit stench of the pot.

Silence flooded into the room as he lowered his gun.

A door creaked open behind him. A loud click broke the calm. "Andrew?"

Pollard's breath caught in his throat. He blinked. *Fuck.* He turned.

Hollister stood there, naked, glassy-eyed, glistening and sweaty. A lopsided grin stretched across her mouth. Traces of cocaine ringed her nostrils. She took a step closer, pressing the nickel-plated .38 in her right hand into his forehead.

Pollard croaked. He wet himself. "Betty..."

Her finger closed on the trigger.

Thirty-Four

A sour-faced man loomed at the foot of Megan's bed, staring at her, frowning. Then he was a woman. No. Two women, with sad eyes. Then a man again, but not the same. Then nothing. No one.

Warmth crept around her thighs and then under, coating her ass, wet, like the ocean in the summer. *It feels good.* Then it became cold, and she hated it. It was morning but it wasn't. *Night. Or is it still morning?*

Again.

Christmas day when she was eight. The blue ornament with baby Jesus on the front. Falling, smashing, and disintegrating. Chloe is crying.

Deep in the recesses of her mind, Megan knew something was wrong, but she couldn't grasp it, couldn't make it stay still long enough to touch, to name. Reality swirled past as if she were a stationary stone in a stream wearing her away bit by bit.

She slept.

~~~

Oh, my God.

"Whu?" Megan slurred, unable to form words through her swollen lips. There was a commotion in the room, the sliding of a chair, the sound of a magazine slapping on tile.

"She's awake!" a woman called out with delight.

Beth? Megan tried to open her eyes, but only succeeded in getting one open partway. Her left eye wouldn't budge. It was glued shut. She felt a cool hand on her forearm.

"It's okay Megan. You're safe now." *Definitely Beth.*

She turned her head to follow the voice, and her friend's concerned face swam into view for a moment before fading away. She felt sick, like she was going to vomit. Bile rose in the back of her throat. She swallowed it back.

"Jack and the doc will be right here," Beth murmured.
~~~

Megan closed her good eye and let herself relax a bit. Her last memory was Pringle's face, a screwed-up mask of malignant fury, and his arm raised high. It had been more terrifying than any zombie she had ever encountered. Everything else was blank. *No. Not quite.* She had snippets of something. Pringle leering at her. This bed. This room, the buzz of cicadas, a cool hand rubbing hers. *This is now.*

Jack and the doctor—*what was his name again? You should know this,* Megan—burst into the room. She attempted a smile and felt her lips crack with the effort. The doctor wore a stethoscope and a flannel shirt, unbuttoned so the curly gray hairs on his chest peeked out. Jack was empty-handed, his hair askew as if he had just risen from a long slumber.

The doctor motioned Beth aside and began to examine Megan. Leaning in close, he pried her left eye open wide with his thumb and forefinger and flashed a light into her pupil.

She whimpered. "Ow…" She could see nothing through the eye, yet the light made the back of her brain burn.

"I'm sorry," the doctor said. "I need to check your concussion." Jack and Beth watched silently though the whole procedure, lifting her limbs and gently replacing them when the doctor asked, taking care not to bump any of her bruises.

"Roll her over, please," the doctor instructed. His name is Steve, Megan remembered. *A veterinarian.* Not a doctor…Jack gave him a questioning look, and then he did as requested.

As they rolled her, her ribs flexed and compressed, sending blinding bolts of pain through her chest. She began to cry. If she had been standing, the pain would have taken her legs right out from under her. She endured another few moments of poking and prodding before the doctor completed his exam with a curt, "Roll her back over, please."

This time, she tried to anticipate the pain, to brace for it, but it was no use. The same agony sliced into her as they returned her to her back. She almost blacked out. Jack leaned in and brushed away a few stray hairs that had slipped into her eye, his touch sending an instant shiver of pleasure through her body, making her forget the pain for a split-second. Megan wiggled her toes, relieved to see they still did what she asked of them.

"How long…?" She tried to ask.

"A week," the doctor replied. She blinked. Tears ran down her cheek. Her throat felt thick with snot. Jack shuffled his feet nervously, as if he didn't know what to say next.

"How am I?" she asked, not able to meet the doctor's eyes. She couldn't bear to see his face if it was bad news.

The doctor cleared his throat. "Considering what you went through, you're in surprisingly good shape. A few broken ribs, a moderate concussion, and your left eye are the only real problems. I haven't detected any signs of internal bleeding, thank God."

Megan swallowed. Their medical facilities were sparse. Major trauma was a death sentence, and would be for the foreseeable future, at least until they found a real doctor and better equipment. She brought her fingers up and probed the swollen skin around her bad eye. She felt a thick line of stitches.

The doctor frowned. "About that..." She understood. The eye was gone.

"What's the last thing you remember?" Jack asked.

"Pringle."

He and Beth shared a quick glance. "Nothing else?"

"Kevin?" she croaked. "Where is he?"

Beth looked at Jack. "He didn't make it."

Megan closed her eye and recited a quick prayer for him. She hadn't known him very well, but he had seemed capable and confident, a solid addition to the community.

"Alicia?" she asked.

Jack answered with a sad shake of his head. "She disappeared that morning. No one has seen her since that day."

"Tell me everything," Megan demanded.

So Jack told her. He started at the point when she, Pringle, and Kevin had disappeared into the building and ended with the moment he found her crumpled on the floor with her life hanging by a thread.

"I can't believe he did this," Megan said in a whisper when he finished.

Jack gave her hand a soft squeeze. "I know. Not now." She wanted to press the point, to get some answers, but she was fading, and all of a sudden, nothing seemed quite as important anymore. Out of the corner of her eye, she noticed the doctor stepping away from her IV with an empty syringe in his hand.

"No..."

But it was too late. Oblivion wrapped her in its soft embrace, and she was gone before she could finish her thought.

Next

Some say the world will end in fire,
Some say in ice.
From what I've tasted of desire
I hold with those who favor fire.
But if it had to perish twice,
I think I know enough of hate
To say that for destruction ice
Is also great
And would suffice.
Robert Frost, Fire and Ice

Thirty-Five

One week later

Megan raised the plastic cup to her mouth and took a sip. She coughed as a stream of lukewarm water went down the wrong pipe. *Ouch.* She winced and touched a hand to her chest. Her ribs ached. No. *Throbbed.* Not as bad as yesterday, thankfully, but not much better.

The doctor had said it would be several weeks before the pain went away, weeks until she healed, weeks until she would feel *normal* again. *Whatever that is.*

She balanced the cup on her knee and stole a glance at Jack. He sat slowly flipping through one of Cesar's notebooks in a leather recliner beside the bed. He murmured to himself, lost in his own bubble of concentration, oblivious to her gaze. Megan took another sip, taking care not to choke this time. A child laughed somewhere outside, and she smiled.

Despite her attempts at learning Jack's story, he somehow managed to always turn the conversation away from himself and back to her, to the community. Something terrible had happened to him, she now realized, something so traumatic it had burned away his capacity for intimacy and left behind a hard, pragmatic core with no capacity for love.

He would heal eventually, she knew. She hoped. In the meantime, she would wait. Still, it pained her to watch him, so strong, yet so distant, trapped inside himself, struggling to exist in a world not of his making. Gone was the shame she had felt the morning before Pringle's attack. Now, when she gazed into Jack's eyes, something she did as often as possible, she was overcome with a sense of calm and strength more powerful than any drug. She was afraid she was falling in love. And the timing couldn't have been worse.

Humanity hung by its fingertips, feet dangling over the precipice of extinction, yet here she was, thinking about this man who had been thrust into her life, dreaming of a future with him despite the staggering odds stacked against them both.

The undead were only a symptom, she had finally realized, a symptom of a broken society that would rather battle each other to the death than compromise for the greater good. It disgusted her.

Megan tried to recall the population of the United States before the collapse. *A few hundred million? Maybe more? How many are left now?* A soft sigh escaped her lips, and she shook her head in sorrow. *It doesn't matter now. It's all gone...*

Megan could handle the undead. As long as they were careful and avoided drawing any swarms to the community, they would survive. But to be challenged by another group of people? That was beyond belief. It violated everything she had ever believed about humanity. In their time of greatest need, it was inconceivable that they would fight amongst themselves, severing the tenuous thread of humanity that connected them all. It was all they had left.

She drew in a deep breath and tried to push the thoughts aside, to focus on her immediate needs, to trust that everything would work out in the end. It was no use. Her heart pounded in her chest. Butterflies fluttered in her stomach. *It's time.*

She unfolded her legs and slid to the edge of the bed. Sensing her movement, Jack looked up.

Megan held out her hand. "Could you help me up? It's time."

He leaped from his chair, put her arm around his shoulder and gently lifted her to her feet.

"Are you sure?"

Megan leaned her head against his neck, feeling the whiskers of his beard brush against her face. "I'm ready..."

Jack raised an eyebrow but didn't argue. His acceptance was unconditional. Arm in arm, they shuffled down the hall and out the door onto the porch. The courtyard was full. It was early, but already hot. People milled about, sticking to the shadows, dodging the late-morning sun.

She slipped from Jack's grasp and patted his shoulder. "I can do this."

"Okay." He stayed close, shadowing her in case her strength faltered.

In halting steps, Megan shuffled to the railing, gripping the warm tubular steel with both hands for support. She steadied herself, her knuckles blanching with the effort. Cords of muscle stood out on her forearms. She stood there for a moment, surveying the community, taking in the mundane bustle of people going about their daily lives.

Across the courtyard a young man noticed her. He stopped. The roll of barbed wire he carried tumbled forgotten to his feet. He called out to a cluster of nearby women and pointed in Megan's direction. Her stomach flip-flopped with anticipation.

Word spread quickly, and within a few minutes, the entire community stood before her. An excited murmur raced through the crowd. People smiled, raising their children on their shoulders and trying to get as close as possible.

Jack's hand brushed her elbow. He whispered, "They need you…"

Megan scanned the crowd; her eyes slid from face to face until they became one. A hush descended. Feet shuffled on asphalt. Gravel crunched underfoot. Biting back her pain, Megan stood as straight as she could. She cleared her throat.

Then, with a final glance over her shoulder at Jack, she began to lay out her plan to reclaim humanity.

About The Author

William Esmont lives in Southern Arizona with his wife and their three dogs and one cat. *Fire* is his third novel. He is currently working on the sequel to his espionage thriller, *The Patriot Paradox,* and sketching out both the sequel and prequel to *Fire.*

If you enjoyed this story, please take a moment to leave a positive review. Good reviews help sell stories, which in return allows William to work less and write more.

If you'd like to contact William, you can reach him thorough the following channels:

Email: *William.Esmont@gmail.com*
Web: *www.WilliamEsmont.com*
Twitter: @*WilliamEsmont*
Facebook: *tinyurl.com/WilliamEsmont-Facebook*

www.ingramcontent.com/pod-product-compliance
Lightning Source LLC
LaVergne TN
LVHW090956080826
845145LV00003B/1029

* 9 7 8 0 9 8 2 8 7 5 8 3 4 *